FOOTBALL FEVER 3

**COLLECTED BY
TONY BRADMAN**

Illustrated by
Jon Riley

CORGI BOOKS

FOOTBALL FEVER 3
A CORGI BOOK : 978 0 552 56733 6

First publication in Great Britain

PRINTING HISTORY
Corgi edition published 2000

3 5 7 9 10 8 6 4 2

Set in Bembo by Phoenix Typesetting, Ilkley, West Yorkshire.

Corgi Books are published by Transworld Publishers,
61-63 Uxbridge Road, London W5 5SA,

Addresses for companies within The Random House Group Limited
can be found at: www.randomhouse.co.uk/offices.htm

The Random House Group Limited supports The Forest Stewardship
Council (FSC®), the leading international forest certification organisation.
Our books carrying the FSC label are printed on FSC® certified paper.
FSC is the only forest certification scheme endorsed by the leading
environmental organisations, including Greenpeace. Our
paper procurement policy can be found at
www.randomhouse.co.uk/environment

MIX
Paper from
responsible sources
FSC® C018072

Printed and bound in Great Britain by Clays Ltd, St Ives PLC

THE SQUAD

THE SQUAD

PAYING THE PRICE
by Narinder Dhami

I had my brilliant idea just after our opponents, Rovers, scored one of the fastest goals in history. Two seconds into the match the ball passed smoothly from one Rovers player to another, without any of the Foxes getting a sniff of it. Some of them didn't even *see* it.

'Tackle them!' I yelled at the Foxes' defence. 'Don't let them set Andy Ball up!'

Andy Ball, known as Cannonball, was the top scorer in the league, and he was lurking with intent on the edge of our box like a hungry shark. The ball dropped invitingly at his feet, and our full-backs, Jaz Patel and Lucy Kelly, obligingly scuttled right out of his way. There was a rumour that a defender who'd tried to block a shot from Andy Ball had ended up with his kidneys relocated near his tonsils. Jaz and Lucy were taking no chances.

Now the only obstacle left was our goalie, Charlie Robson, who'd never saved a one-on-one shot yet. As Charlie blinked in a bemused way behind his owlish specs, Andy drove the ball hard and low into the bottom left-hand corner of the net. A second later, Charlie dived, mis-timed it and clunked his head on the goal post. He did that so regularly I'd suggested he wear a cycle helmet.

'Oh, well done, lads!' called Charlie's dad, looking up quickly. He had his head down, marking essays as usual.

'We didn't score, sir,' I said. 'They did.'

'Oh. Right.' Mr Robson looked momentarily flustered.

I sighed, and glanced at Alex Brennan who partnered me up front and was my best mate. Robbo's our manager. He's a history teacher at the Comp, and he knows as much about football as I do about flower-arranging, but we've got to have an adult around or we can't compete in the league. If you can call it competing.

Rovers already had the ball back at the centre circle, and were hunched over it like vultures in for the kill.

'Jaz! Lucy!' I dashed over to our backs. 'You've got to start marking Andy Ball!'

'But he's *scary*,' Jaz said, his bottom lip quivering.

'Don't give me that!' I snapped. 'What are you, football players or wimps?'

Jaz and Lucy looked at each other as if they weren't quite sure.

I don't know why I was getting so wound up. The league wasn't anything special. It had been started years ago by the local youth centre to give kids something to do on Sunday mornings, and it had always been a bit disorganized. It was only supposed to be a bit of a laugh, a chance to have a kick-around with your mates in the park on a Sunday morning. But things were changing fast.

Some of the teams had bought their own flashy matching kits while the rest of us were still playing in a mixture of tracksuits and Premiership football strips. The top team, the Eagles, were rumoured to train hard three times a week. And there was even talk of going to the FA and the local sports authority and getting the league made official. Then I'd be captain of *officially* the worst team in the district. Excellent.

I could see the second goal coming a mile off. One of the Rovers' players collected the ball and chipped it right over everyone's heads to Andy Ball. Andy timed his run perfectly, ensuring that he was on-side when the ball landed at his feet, before banging it into the net.

'Sorry, Jonno,' Charlie called sheepishly. 'I wasn't ready.'

'Don't worry about it, Charlie.' I didn't add that Andy Ball could have run down the pitch holding a placard saying I AM NOW GOING TO TAKE A SHOT AT GOAL, and Charlie still wouldn't have been ready.

Personally, I didn't need the aggro. I played for my school team on Saturday mornings, and we were top of the junior schools league. But I'd always wanted to play for the Foxes. My big sister Lauren had actually started the team years ago, and she was an ace player. The Foxes had won the league five times in a row. But this lot couldn't win a cup of tea. Apart from Alex and me, they were unfit, bored and demoralized. Every week one or two of them didn't turn up, and Alex and I had to run round the park trying to find substitutes. Today we had a seven-year-old kid who'd been walking his dog playing for us. You're supposed to be between nine and eleven years old to play in the league. I had to tell the ref he was a late developer.

Rovers had finished celebrating their second goal. They were now strolling back to the centre circle with the smug faces of those who knew that they were going to boost their goal average significantly by the end of the match. They were second in the league to the Eagles. The Foxes were bottom. We'd played 10, won 0, drawn 0, lost 10, goals for 0, goals against 78.

Yes, 78.

I was seriously fed up. This wasn't why I'd joined the Foxes. I didn't expect to win every week, but once a season would be good. Not all the team were hopeless players, but no-one had any confidence, and Robbo was kind-hearted but useless.

The supporters weren't much help either. Lauren had given up coming to watch. She said she couldn't take that much tragedy on a regular basis. Alex's dad was here as usual, but he was so bored, he was reading the *Daily Mirror*. It was when I saw the headline on the back page that I stopped dead. It read MANCHESTER UNITED IN TRANSFER BID FOR JUVENTUS STAR, and *that* was when I had my excellent idea.

'Hey, Andy.'

I'd hung around after the match, waiting for Cannonball to come out. I hadn't told any of the other Foxes my plan, though. Not even Alex.

'Hey, Jonno.' Andy's round face broke into a smug grin. 'How does it feel to have your backside kicked?'

I managed a smile. 'Not good, actually.'

The final score had been 11–0, and Andy Ball had scored ten goals. The Rovers' goalie, Kevin Radford, had scored the last one five minutes from the end. Apparently he'd got bored standing in goal, doing nothing. Then he'd gone over to chat with a mate who was standing in the crowd. We *still* hadn't managed to score.

'Anyway,' I went on as Andy unwrapped a Crunchie and scoffed it in four bites, 'I want to talk to you.'

Andy took out a Twix. 'Yeah?'

'How would you feel about joining the Foxes?'

Andy almost choked. 'Do *what*?'

'We'd like you to transfer to the Foxes,' I told him.

'A *transfer* to the *Foxes*?' Andy began to roar with laughter. Transfers were virtually unknown in the

11

league, although there were no rules restricting which clubs you could play for. But people tended to want to stick with their mates, so no-one really moved around. 'Are you off your trolley, Jonno? Transfer to the Foxes? You're bottom of the league!'

'But we wouldn't be if we had *you* playing for us,' I pointed out.

Andy stopped laughing. 'You've got a flippin' nerve, Jonno!' he exclaimed self-righteously. 'Why should I leave all my mates in the Rovers to play for your rubbish team? I wouldn't leave the Rovers if *we* were bottom of the league, and the Foxes were at the top! I'm a Rovers man for life!'

''Course, we'd make it worth your while,' I said, playing my trump card.

'What?' Andy Ball stopped in mid-rant.

'We'd offer you incentives.'

'In-what?' Andy Ball might be a great striker, but he wasn't exactly the sharpest tool in the box.

'Incentives. Little extras.' I nearly said 'bribes', but that sounded a bit too near the knuckle.

'Oh, you mean bribes,' Andy said, his eyes gleaming with avarice. 'Like what?'

I glanced at the crumpled wrapper in his hand. 'Five bars of the chocolate of your choice after every match.' I paused for effect. 'Whether we win or lose.'

'Yeah?' Andy was impressed, I could tell.

'So, are you up for it?'

Andy grinned. 'Five bars of chocolate *and* two bags

of cheese and onion crisps. And they've got to be Walkers, you know, like Michael Owen.'

I nodded and held out my hand. 'It's a deal.'

'Family-sized bags,' Andy added quickly. He might not be very bright, but he was learning fast. I grabbed his hand before he could ask for a Big Mac and large fries too, and we shook.

'See you at training on Wednesday,' I called, as he went off down the street, unwrapping a Snickers bar. I waited until he was out of sight. Only then did I punch the air, and shout '*YES!*'

I couldn't wait to see the Foxes' faces when Andy 'Cannonball' Ball turned up for training next week.

'But I don't *get* it!' Alex said for the twentieth time.

I dribbled my ball faster round the cones, trying to get away from him, but Alex just dribbled faster too and caught me up. 'Why does Andy Ball want to play for *us*?'

'He just decided that he wanted a transfer, all right?' I replied shortly. I hadn't told Alex about the 'incentives'. I had a feeling he might think I'd gone too far. 'What's your problem?'

The sensation that Andy Ball's arrival at our training session had caused was almost as great as if Alan Shearer himself had turned up. I always had to bully the Foxes into turning up, but this time I'd told them I'd got a surprise for them so they were all out in force. Andy had been very gratified by all the attention, and was now strutting round the pitch in his expensive track-suit, doing ball tricks. The other Foxes were standing round watching him, open-mouthed, while Mr Robson stood at the side, marking madly.

'What do you mean, a *transfer*?' Alex persisted, following me in and out of the line of cones. 'This isn't the Premiership!'

'Look, I asked Andy if he wanted to transfer to the Foxes, and he said yes.' That was all I was going to say. Alex actually has a conscience, which can be kind of inconvenient in a best mate.

'So what did you offer him then?' Alex asked casually.

'Five bars of chocolate and two packets of crisps.' I turned bright red. 'I wasn't going to tell you that.'

'I bet.' Alex gave me an angry shove, and I nearly impaled myself on a plastic cone. 'What did you go and do a stupid thing like that for?'

'Oh, so it's *stupid* to get good players for the Foxes, is it?' I shot back angrily.

'Yeah, it is, if you have to bribe them!' Alex retorted. 'Andy's a Rovers man. He hasn't got any loyalty to the Foxes.'

'So? What about all the players in the Premiership who change clubs?' I pointed out. '*They're* loyal to their new teams.'

'Premiership players get a bit more than five bars of chocolate and two packets of crisps when they transfer clubs,' Alex said drily.

'Look,' I told him, 'we're playing the Eagles next Sunday and, for once, we've got a chance of not making complete prats of ourselves. What's so wrong about that?'

Alex shrugged, and dribbled his ball away again. I pulled a face at his back. He could be a right pain sometimes. Well, we'd see what he had to say after the match against the Eagles next Sunday morning . . .

'What did you say about not making complete prats of ourselves?' Alex mouthed at me, as the Eagles celebrated their sixteenth goal. Their star midfield player, Emily Barrett, had collected a pass from their captain, Gary Rogers, and then curled a fantastic shot into the net. The ball had flown through the air in a banana-shaped curve, nearly taking Charlie Robson's cycle helmet with it.

Things had started off pretty well. I was partnering Andy up front, and Alex had dropped back into midfield. For once, everyone in the Foxes, excited by the Andy Ball transfer, had turned up for the match.

So the Foxes had trooped out onto the pitch in a new spirit of comradeship and confidence. That had lasted for five minutes, until Eagles' striker Terry Phillips had scored their first goal.

I ignored Alex and dashed back into the Eagles' half, where Andy Ball was yawning and kicking at a daisy.

'Come on, Andy!' I said urgently. 'Let's stop them getting another one at least!'

Andy shrugged. 'Sorry, I don't do defending.'

'But—'

Andy looked at me stubbornly. 'I don't do defending,' he repeated. 'You get the ball down to me, and I'll score. That's *my* job.'

I stared at him, my heart sinking. I realized what a bad mistake I'd made. Andy Ball wasn't a grafter. Instead he sat back and waited for the ball to come to him. Well, that might be all right with the Rovers team behind him, but he'd wait till Christmas for the Foxes to deliver.

'You'd better get this sorted out, mate.' Andy was kicking savagely at his daisy. 'I've hardly touched the ball!'

'You took a throw-in,' I reminded him desperately.

Andy glared at me. 'I mean with my *feet*. I want to be the highest goal-scorer again this year, and if you don't start giving me some service, I'm out of here!'

There was only one answer, obviously. What the Foxes needed was a class midfielder to feed Andy Ball, someone who could score goals as well as create them. We were playing the Eagles again in two weeks' time, and by then I was going to have the Foxes sorted out if it killed me. As the ref blew the final whistle, I dashed over to shake hands with Emily Barrett.

'Great game, Emily,' I said. 'Can I talk to you later? I've got a little proposition to put to you . . .'

★   ★   ★

'You were talking to Emily Barrett for a long time yesterday,' Alex said as we walked to school on Monday morning.

'So?' I scowled. 'It's not a crime, is it?'

Alex didn't say anything. But it didn't take me very long to crack.

'All right! I asked her if she wanted to join the Foxes.'

'Another transfer?' Alex raised his eyebrows. 'I can't see Emily leaving the Eagles for five bars of chocolate and two bags of crisps.'

'No.' I scowled again. 'She wants £2.50 for every game. And an extra pound for every goal she scores.'

'Big bucks, huh?' Alex frowned. 'Can you afford it?'

'Just about. Anyway, she hasn't said yes yet. She said she wanted to think about it—'

I stopped. Emily Barrett and another girl I didn't know were walking purposefully towards us. It looked like I was about to clinch my second big transfer deal.

'Hi, Emily,' I said eagerly, 'have you thought about what I said yesterday?'

'Emily still needs a little more time to think about it.' said the other girl.

'I wasn't talking to you,' I said.

'Well, you'd better.' The girl fixed me with a steely stare. 'Emily's asked me to negotiate for her.'

'What?' I looked at Emily, who stared back at me, unsmiling. 'Has she suddenly lost the power of speech or something?'

The girl ignored that. 'I'm Danielle Lewis, Emily's

best mate. And I have to say I'm not that impressed with the deal you're offering.'

'What!' I spluttered.

'Well, £2.50 per match isn't much for a player of Emily's ability,' Danielle pointed out coolly. 'We think she should be getting a fiver at least.'

'No way!'

'Fine.' Danielle shrugged. 'But I have to warn you that Emily's had another offer.'

'Another offer?' I was dismayed. News of my transfer activity must have started to leak out. 'Who from?'

'I can't say.' Danielle folded her arms. 'But they're prepared to pay what we're asking, *and* provide an unlimited supply of jam doughnuts.'

Emily nudged Danielle and whispered in her ear.

'However, Emily might reconsider,' Danielle went on, 'if you were willing to match that, *and* offer something extra.'

'Like what?' I asked.

'Well, Emily fancies a personal cheerleading squad,' Danielle explained. 'You know, good-looking boys with pom-poms chanting her name. E-M-I-L-Y. That kind of thing.'

I stared at the two girls. They were *serious*.

'Emily would need to approve all the boys personally, of course,' Danielle added.

'Of course,' I repeated, dazed.

'We'll leave it with you then.' Danielle nodded briskly at me, then they walked off.

'Do you *believe* what just happened?' I asked Alex.

'You've really gone and done it now, Jonno.' Alex shook his head. 'The transfer market's gone barking mad!'

Alex was right. I'd really started something in the league. The next thing we heard was that Kevin Radford, the Rovers' goalie, had been offered a pet gerbil and a pair of second-hand roller blades to move to the Tigers, Kelly Preston had gone from the Downtowners to Rovers (salt and vinegar crisps, and a poster of Boyzone), and Luke Page had transferred from Riverside to the Panthers (a *Match of the Day* video and a regular supply of Cadbury's chocolate buttons).

And so it went on.

The next match came and went. We lost 14–0 to the Lions and Andy Ball sulked furiously, but the rest of the Foxes hardly noticed. They were buzzing with the news that the Eagles' striker Terry Phillips had been tempted away by the Tigers, with the promise of a £5 bonus every time he scored. Meanwhile, Danielle Lewis was still bringing me increasingly outrageous requests from Emily Barrett for her own private dressing room (with her name in gold letters on the door), and a cup of hot chocolate at half-time when it was chilly.

It was really frustrating. The transfers had been *my* idea, and where had it got us? Nowhere. With all the other clubs muscling in, we didn't have a hope of matching the incentives they were offering. The only thing we still had was Andy Ball . . .

I was leaving our training session on Wednesday when I suddenly spotted Andy talking to Gary Rogers, the Eagles' captain, and Mark Davis, their centre-half. I was instantly suspicious.

'Hey, Gary!' I called, as soon as Andy had sauntered off, grinning widely. I wanted to find out exactly what was going down.

'Hey, Jonno,' Gary said. 'How's things?'

'That depends on what you and Andy Ball were just talking about,' I said grimly.

Gary shrugged. 'Sorry, mate. He's decided to transfer to the Eagles.'

'What're you paying him?' I asked wearily.

'A Big Mac and large fries, four times a week,' Mark replied.

So now we didn't even have Andy Ball.

'What about you then, Jonno?' Gary glanced slyly at me. 'Do you fancy playing for the Eagles yourself?'

I blinked. '*What?*'

'We need another striker,' Mark chimed in. 'We can offer you Coca-Cola at half-time, kit hand-washed weekly by my mum *with* generous amounts of fabric conditioner, and—'

'But you've got Jamie Robinson,' I broke in.

'Nah, he's transferred to the Tigers with Terry,' Gary said.

'For an Everton scarf and a *Blue Peter* annual,' Mark

said bitterly. 'That boy's got no class.'

'But I haven't scored this season.' I didn't know why I was being so awkward. I'd *always* wanted to play for the top team. I'd just hoped the top team would be the Foxes.

'Yeah, but you're not getting the service, are you?' Gary pointed out. 'Come on, Jonno, what do you say?'

I was speechless. It was a chance in a million. But it meant leaving Alex and the other Foxes behind.

'You can play for us on Sunday,' Mark suggested, but the thought turned my stomach. I couldn't play my first game for the Eagles against the Foxes.

'No,' I said quickly. 'I'll think about it and let you know after the match . . .'

'What's up?' Alex stared at me as the Foxes straggled gloomily out of the changing rooms. Andy Ball's defection had hit them hard. 'You've got a face on you like I don't know what.'

'I'm just not looking forward to another pasting,' I replied quickly. I glanced round, surprised to see that the Eagles weren't out yet. The Foxes, reluctant to face further humiliation, were *always* last on the pitch. Not today, though.

The Eagles came out just then, looking rather disorganized. Because of all the mad transfer activity they had about five new players, who were looking as if they weren't quite sure what they were doing there. Not only that, Emily Barrett and Mark Davis were arguing loudly.

'Well, I've had five offers, so there!' Emily was saying snootily. 'I just haven't decided which one to go with yet.'

'So? I've got *six* clubs after me!' Mark retorted. 'I've been offered ten quid a week to play for Riverside!'

'Will you two shut up!' Gary Rogers hissed at them.

'Just because no-one's asked *you* to play for them!' Emily snorted, and Gary looked livid.

Alex nudged me. 'Hey, what happened to Cannonball?'

Andy was living up to his nickname. He looked much rounder, and the Eagles shirt he was wearing hardly fitted him.

'Too much junk food, I reckon!' I whispered back.

Alex and I lined up in the centre to kick off the Cup match. I remembered this might be the very last time I played for the Foxes, and a stupid lump popped up into my throat. But I deserved the chance to play for the top team, didn't I? Anyone would do the same . . . .

As the ref blew the whistle, I played the ball to Alex, and set off towards the Eagles' goal. Alex wrong-footed Gary Rogers, who was still sulking, pushed forward and then stroked the ball back to me. I could hear Emily Barrett and Mark Davis still arguing, and I half-expected one of them to challenge me. They didn't: I looked round as I ran, and realized with a shock that I was unmarked. The full-backs, who were both new, were caught on the hop. I had a clear run into the penalty area.

My vision narrowed until all I could see was the Eagles' goal. The goalie came out to try and block my shot, but that didn't put me off. I dummied the ball neatly past him, and blasted it into the empty goal. The Foxes had scored.

There was dead silence for a moment. Then there was a roar that sounded as loud as Wembley Stadium – to me, anyway. And suddenly I was crushed by the weight of ten bodies landing on top of me.

'You scored!' Alex yelled in my ear.

'We're winning!' shrieked Lucy Kelly, who was sitting on my left leg.

'We're actually winning!' babbled Charlie Robson, bouncing up and down on my stomach.

All right, so we weren't winning because we were a good side. I knew it was because half the Eagles' players were new, the other half were arguing bitterly and Andy Ball was stuffed to the brim with junk food. But it still felt *good*.

'Right!' I pushed everyone off, and got to my feet. 'Listen to me, you lot – we're going to win this!'

Alex nodded, but the other Foxes looked alarmed.

'Hey, steady on, Jonno!' Charlie gasped.

'Yeah, don't get carried away!' Jaz Patel added.

'Look, we can do it!' I said urgently. 'I don't know about you, but I'm fed up with being a permanent joke. Let's kick someone else's backsides for a change!'

A ragged cheer went up from the Foxes. Their eyes were shining, and they had the smell of battle in their

nostrils. I had a feeling that, this time, they wouldn't let the side down.

There wasn't much point in Gary Rogers and Mark Davis asking me what I'd decided after the match finished. It was obvious. The Foxes had won 2–0, and we carried on celebrating long after the Eagles had trudged gloomily off the pitch, still arguing.

The Eagles had gone to pieces after we'd scored in the first minute, despite their manager (Gary Rogers's dad) yelling himself hoarse from the touchline. We'd hit them with another goal just before half-time, scored by Barry Sullivan. It was a bit of a fluke because it had gone in off the back of his neck, but Barry had been thrilled. He'd played like a demon after that.

Half the Eagles' players had sulked, Andy Ball had spent most of the game wheezing and all the new players had decided to return to their old clubs. I had a feeling that the same thing was probably happening at all the matches that morning. In fact, I wouldn't be surprised if *everyone* ended up going back to their old clubs.

'Hey, Jonno.' Alex came over to shake hands with me yet again. 'Great game!'

'Yeah.' I hesitated, then decided to come clean. 'You know, the Eagles asked me to join them . . .'

'Yeah?' Alex stared at me coldly. 'You were going to leave the Foxes?'

'I was thinking about it . . .' I admitted guiltily.

Alex's face broke into a grin. 'I was going to tell you after the match – Rovers asked me for a transfer!'

I chucked one of my shinpads at him as he ran off. Now I had *big* plans for the Foxes. We'd find ourselves some more decent players, and not by nicking them from other clubs either. We'd go scouting for them. And we'd find a new manager too, and let Robbo off the hook. One who knew their penalty area from their centre circle . . .

Someone slapped me hard on the back. 'Nice one, Jonno!' said a familiar voice, and I spun round.

'Lauren!' It was my sister. 'I didn't know you were here!'

Lauren grinned at me. 'Well, I've been hearing some pretty strange stories, so I thought I'd better come and check them out!'

'Er – yeah. The transfer deals.' I turned pink. 'They – er – didn't exactly work out.'

Lauren shrugged. 'Well, it looks like you might have the makings of a half-decent team anyway.'

'Maybe, if we could just get a good manager . . .' And then it hit me. 'Hey, why don't *you* manage us?'

'No way!' Lauren had started shaking her head before the question was out of my mouth. 'I'm too busy with college, and I've got my part-time job at the burger bar—'

'I could offer you some incentives,' I broke in slyly. 'Your old banger – I mean, your car cleaned every week, I'll do the washing-up at home when it's your turn *and* you can have my signed Manchester United team photo! What do you say?'

Lauren was already weakening. I could see it in her eyes.

'Well . . .'

'Great!' I held out my hand. 'It's a deal!'

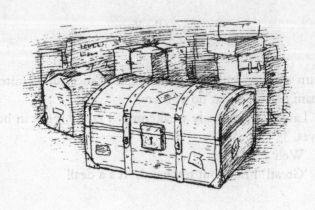

INJURY TIME
by Nick Gifford

'Of course I want to play,' said Andy Biggs to his two friends, as they stood outside the school gates. 'But I can't, can I?'

He dragged the old tennis ball back under his foot and flipped it up with the toe of a Nike Ultracell trainer. Onto the right foot again. Right. Left. Left again, the ball never touching the ground.

'But it's the final,' said Ben, as if Andy didn't already know that.

On Saturday morning it was the final of the County Challenge Trophy and Andy should be playing for the local youth team. He kicked the ball high into the air and watched it back down onto his knee. 'Dad says I have to help him with Mr Bentley's boat,' he said.

'I can't get out of it. He can hardly launch it on his own, can he?'

'But it's not just a game,' said Tony. 'There's supposed to be a scout coming from Borough – just looking for players like us!'

'Says who?' Left foot, left again. Right.

'Says everyone,' Ben answered. 'It could be your big chance, Andy.' Borough were back in the Premiership this year – they might even avoid relegation if they could put a few results together.

Right foot again, then another high one onto the head, the left foot, the left again.

'I told you,' said Andy. 'I don't have any choice.' He flicked the ball up, watched it rise, hang for an instant, fall . . . and kicked it hard and low along the street.

The *Standard* was on the front door mat when Andy reached home. He picked up the paper and turned it over as he shut the door behind him.

There was a paragraph on the back about Saturday's final, more on the inside back page.

He sat down at the kitchen table, his heart racing. He opened the paper. There was a single column on the inside back page, previewing the final: Bathside Youth v Wakering.

'Oh no,' he groaned when he spotted his own name in the second paragraph: '. . . *leading the way for Bathside will be midfield dynamo Andy Biggs, hoping for another goal to keep up his record of scoring in every round.'*

Oh no he won't, thought Andy. Not when Dad sees this.

Andy's father wouldn't let him play football. He hated the game – he said it was pointless, that it took over people's lives. He'd even stopped him from playing for the school team. Andy remembered the letter his father had written: '*My son, Andy Biggs, is not to play football outside formal PE lessons,*' it had said.

Andy closed the paper, wondering what he could do. On the back there was a story about Borough.

Just then his father came in through the back door. He'd been working at the allotment and now he kicked one muddy boot off, then stooped awkwardly to remove the other.

Andy grunted a greeting.

His father came to sit at the table, one leg stretched out straight. He scowled when he saw that Andy was reading the sports pages.

'The knee bad today, is it?' asked Andy. It always was when his father had been digging.

His father nodded. 'I need a bath,' he said. 'Give it a good soak. You still on to cook the tea, are you?'

Andy nodded. Then he said, 'Are you sure you'll be up to launching Mr Bentley's yacht on Saturday? Can't we leave it a bit?'

His father had been preparing to pull himself out of his seat, but now he paused. 'I'll be OK,' he said. 'Especially with your help, eh? And anyway, Terry

Bentley's paying good money to have the *Lady Jane* spruced up. I can't afford to mess this up now, can I?'

'It's only . . . Can't we do it another day? Sunday, maybe?'

'Why's that? What are you planning?'

'I . . . oh nothing. I just . . .'

'There's nothing else to do on Saturday, is there?' said his father. 'Nothing worth your time.' Then he narrowed his eyes and added, 'You weren't thinking of sneaking off to play that game again, were you? Wasting your time kicking a bag of air around a field, just waiting for someone twice your size to do the same to *you*.'

Andy knew he was blushing. He couldn't help it. He looked away, shook his head. 'I just . . .'

I just wish I could explain what it *means* to me, he thought, but he couldn't say it.

He went over to the cupboard, found a bag of potatoes and tipped them into the sink. He reached for the radio and turned it on: an old one from Oasis, 'Roll With It'. He turned it up loud and, ever so casually, took the back page of the paper to catch the potato peelings.

Andy had been coming to his grandparents for tea every Wednesday ever since his mother had left, three years back.

He put his cup back in its saucer and said, 'Can I look in The Box again, Grandad?'

They went through to the back bedroom, where his grandparents kept books and photo albums and spare furniture and even an old bike that couldn't have been ridden since about 1973. And boxes – everywhere, boxes.

But The Box was different. It wasn't really a box at all. It was wooden, with ridged metal bands around it and a hefty metal lock that wouldn't quite lock. It was more of a chest – a treasure chest.

Grandad dragged The Box out into the open, then stood back to let Andy raise the lid.

On top was an old pair of Adidas boots. The studs had been unscrewed and placed in a brown paper bag stuffed into the left boot. Andy lifted the boots out, then a white shirt with blue and red trim, three lions on the chest.

Underneath were some trophies, an FA Cup-winner's Medal, a single, gold-tasselled England Under-21 cap.

And beneath them all: a large leather-bound scrap-book.

Andy glanced at Grandad, then lifted the book out and placed it on the floor. If you looked at the scrap-book edge-on you could see the pages where something had been stuck in: the paper was spaced out, warped. And you could see the flat, tightly packed pages that had not been used.

The book stopped less than halfway through.

Andy flicked through the familiar pages, full of

yellowed newspaper cuttings from the 1970s, and just into the 1980s.

There was a picture of a young star, Kevin Biggs, scoring the winning goal in a cup-tie for Spurs. Another showed Kevin Biggs sitting high on the shoulders of his teammates, with the lid of the FA Cup perched precariously on his head. Andy recognized Ossie Ardiles, and that other Argentinian . . . Ricky Villa.

Andy stared at the pictures of his father and wondered what it must have been like.

'He was just like you,' said Grandad, from the doorway. 'He was fast, but his brain made him even faster. He was a slow developer and when he was your age his teammates were all six inches taller. But he made up for that with his speed and with the way he could read a game. Are you ready for the big game, Andy?'

Andy kept his head down. 'Dad wants me to help him launch Mr Bentley's yacht,' he said. 'He's chosen Saturday just to stop me playing, I reckon.'

He turned over another page and found a place where there was just a loose newspaper cutting. His grandparents hadn't stuck it down. After that the book was empty.

He unfolded the cutting. The photograph showed his father on crutches, one leg in plaster. IT'S ALL OVER, shouted the headline. Underneath, in smaller print, it said, SPURS STAR OUT OF ENGLAND SQUAD – AND OUT OF FOOTBALL.

'Your dad has a lot of problems with the game,' said

Grandad. 'It hurt him – and I don't just mean the knee. A sliding tackle, a bad landing with his leg twisted under him, and it was all over. All his dreams were shattered. He'd always been Kevin Biggs, the footballer. It took him a long time to learn how to be just plain Kevin Biggs.'

Andy wasn't sure his father had learnt that even now. When the injury had stopped him playing he had drifted from one hopeless job to another – he could never stick with anything. Dad hated it when people didn't know who he was, but he hated it even more when they *did*. Even nowadays, people sometimes came up to him and said, 'Hey, didn't you used to be a footballer?' Eventually, his endless moods had even driven Andy's long-suffering mother away. She lived in Cardiff now, with a new job and a new family. Andy visited her whenever it could be arranged, but it never felt right.

Andy's father blamed football for everything that had gone wrong with his life. Now, it seemed that he hated the game with the same intensity that Andy loved it.

'He doesn't have to take it out on me,' Andy muttered.

'He doesn't want you to be hurt like he was,' said Grandad. 'He may be wrong, but he's only trying to do his best.'

Andy shrugged. He didn't want to argue with Grandad. After all, if it wasn't for him, Andy wouldn't even have had a chance to play in the first place: it was

34

Grandad who had tried to persuade Andy's father to change his mind. Later, it was Grandad who had taken Andy along to Bathside Youth, Grandad who had talked to the coach and filled in Andy's registration form.

'I know,' said Andy. But knowing didn't make it any easier to deal with.

When he got home that night, Andy poked his head around the door of the front room to let his father know he was back.

His father was in his chair, staring at the TV without really watching it. His features were a lot rounder than they had been in all the pictures, his hair shorter. He didn't really look like the same man at all. A brother, or cousin, maybe.

He said hello to Andy, then looked up again, and added, 'Oh yes. I nearly forgot. Saturday's off, Andy. I've had a change of plan. We'll do the yacht on Sunday if that's OK with you.'

Andy shrugged, fighting hard not to show his delight. *Yes!* He could play in the final!

On the Friday after school a small group played headers and volleys on the recreation ground.

'Go on!' Andy had chipped it up for Wicksy, but the header went straight into Stu's arms in goal.

'Getting nervous, are you?' said Ben, when the ball went over to the other side of the field. 'Butterflies in the old stomach, eh?'

35

Andy shrugged. 'Not about the game,' he said. It was the biggest game he'd ever played in, but he knew he was ready for it. 'It's all the other stuff,' he said. 'It'll be in the *Standard*. Photos on the back page and all that. No way will I be able to keep *that* from Dad. He'll find out I've been playing. He'll probably find out that Grandad's been helping me and they'll have another of their arguments. And no more football for me.'

Wicksy put a long ball in from the touchline, but no-one was near enough to do anything with it. Andy jogged over and lobbed the ball into the middle for Tony to volley into the goal.

'You just have to impress the scout then,' said Ben. 'Sign up with Borough and there's nothing your dad can do to stop you.'

But Andy knew it wasn't so simple. He'd never be able to sign schoolboy papers with Borough without his father's permission.

On Saturday morning Andy was about to leave for the match when he saw that his father was about to go out, too.

'Where are you off to, Dad?' he asked.

'There's a football match,' his father said. 'A kids' game. County final or something. Grandad persuaded me to have a look. He says there are some good players. I thought I'd go along and see how the game's changed since my day.'

Andy stared at his father, then made himself turn away before his expression gave away his shock. 'See you, then,' he mumbled.

His father went out of the front door.

Dad never went to football matches.

Never.

He hadn't been to a game since the day his career had been ended by a single badly timed tackle.

He hated football.

So why was he going today, of all days?

Andy watched out of the landing window as his father limped down the street. At the end he turned left instead of right – away from the ground. Maybe he wasn't going after all!

But then Andy realized that he must be going to meet Grandad, and the two would go together. This must be another of Grandad's schemes to make everything better, but Andy knew his father could never be persuaded. If he saw Andy running out onto that pitch he'd go ballistic!

Andy fetched his bag and left for the ground. What was he going to do?

'Hey, Biggsy! You made it!'

The dressing room was full of teenagers in varying stages of undress. Andy saw a space on one of the benches: the black and white strip of Bathside Youth had been laid out neatly, ready for him.

Mr Wilson, the team's coach, came across to meet

him. 'Trouble?' he said straight away, reading the look on Andy's face.

Andy nodded. 'It's Dad,' he said. 'He's coming to the match.'

'Hey, that's great, isn't it?'

Andy shook his head. Coach knew his father had problems with the game, but he didn't realize quite how bad things were. 'I can't play,' Andy said. 'Dad'll go mad if he sees me out there.'

Coach opened his mouth to speak, then stopped. 'Andy,' he started again, 'are you telling me you're pulling out of the final?'

Andy looked around the silent dressing room. They were all watching him. They wanted him to play. 'I . . .'

He thought of his father, standing out there in the crowd. At least he'd be with Grandad – maybe that would calm him down a bit.

Maybe it was time he stood up for himself. Time to make his own decisions.

'I'll play,' he said quietly.

The cheers from the dressing room could probably be heard on the other side of town.

The crowd was big for a youth game – over 300, Coach had told them. 'And most of them want Bathside Youth to lift that cup. Don't let them down.'

Andy kept his head down during the warm-up. He tried to concentrate on the match ahead, tried to remember everything Coach had told them about the opposition. They're big, but that makes them slow. They play solid and flat across the back and they knock lots of long balls up into the final third of the pitch.

When the teams lined up for the kick-off, Andy glanced around the crowd but he couldn't see his father.

Ben tapped the kick-off to Wicksy, who instantly rolled it back to Andy.

Andy trapped the ball, held it for an instant to allow Ben to make his usual run for the right flank.

But he held it for just too long. Their big centre-forward charged him down, took the ball from Andy's feet and knocked him to the ground.

Andy lay for a few seconds in the mud. The ball had gone into touch.

He hadn't been concentrating. He hadn't been ready.

He scrambled to his feet, ran back to support the back four.

The throw was long and hopeful. Richie cleared the ball, but only as far as one of the Wakering players, who knocked it straight back in. After a bit of a scrap in the penalty area, the ball rolled away for a goal kick. Stu fetched the ball and took his time placing it, calming things down.

He kicked high over Andy's head towards Wicksy.

Andy turned, watching the ball, and then his eye caught someone in the crowd – his father staring at him, a grim expression on his face.

Next to him, Grandad was shouting, waving a hand, but Andy couldn't take his eyes off his father. He couldn't work out what that expression said. The only thing he knew for sure was that his secret was out.

Before Andy could get his mind back on the game their number seven had gone past him with the ball.

This was probably going to be his last game, he realized. He twisted, chased the player.

He caught him quickly and slid in at an angle.

He had to time it perfectly or he'd take the player out and give away a free kick.

Right foot stretching, toe down so the studs don't show . . .

He made contact with the ball, sent it flying into touch. The number seven went down, but it was a fair tackle and the ref signalled the throw.

Andy was up on his feet instantly, pulling his opponent up from the ground.

The ball had gone into the crowd. At first Andy couldn't see where it had gone, then he saw that his father was holding it, staring at it.

It was probably the first time he had touched a football in nearly twenty years.

For a moment Andy thought he was going to hang on to it, then Grandad leaned over and said something. When Andy's father still did nothing, Grandad took the ball from his hands and threw it back onto the pitch.

Andy turned away.

He wondered when his father had realized Andy was

playing. Had Grandad told him before the match? Had he guessed even earlier than that?

Andy felt certain, now, that this would be his last game. Let's make it one to remember, he thought.

He backed away from the throw. He thought over what Grandad had said about his father: 'He was fast, but his brain made him even faster.'

The ball was probably going to go down to the corner of the box, where their number four was trying to pull away from Richie.

Andy was running a split second ahead of the throw.

He made it easily, held the ball up for a second, then played a long, angled pass across to Wicksy, who was waiting in space on the halfway line. 'Play it to feet and keep moving,' Coach had told them.

Their right-back took Wicksy out with a crunching tackle and the ref blew for a free kick. Andy ran up to take it.

It was going to be a long, hard game.

Half an hour into the second half and still there was no score.

Bathside Youth had tried to keep to Coach's instructions, but Wakering were a hard team to open up. Andy was going to have a lot of bruises by tomorrow.

He'd spent most of the game sitting back in midfield, stealing the ball, sending out a succession of sharp passes, trying to keep things moving. But he wasn't used to this

41

kind of hard, physical game. It wasn't his style.

He hadn't exactly done much wrong, but not much had gone *right*, either.

And then Ben picked up the ball out on the right, just inside the Wakering half. He had space, and he ran with it down the line.

Two of their defenders saw what was happening and they ran at him.

And that meant they had left a gap.

Andy drifted upfield until he was nearly level with their last player.

He waited, waited.

He knew Ben had seen him and was just waiting for the right moment to pass.

Andy didn't even watch him, he just waited for the sound of foot on ball.

Thud.

Ben had played it on into the gap and instantly Andy sprinted through.

He was in open space, just the keeper to beat. He dummied then drove it low, under the keeper's hand.

The whistle blew.

Andy turned.

The ref was disallowing the goal: offside.

Ben started to argue, but there was no point. Referees don't change their minds, even when they're wrong. Andy put an arm across his friend's chest and turned him away. 'Come on, Ben,' he said. 'We'll just have to do it again.'

*   *   *

But they didn't.

A few minutes after Andy's disallowed goal the Wakering keeper kicked a long ball up into Bathside's penalty area. Their centre-forward shouldered Richie out of the way and drove it into the corner of the net.

1–0. And that was how it stayed.

It was only when they trudged off the pitch that Andy remembered the rumour about the scout from Borough. He hadn't even thought about it all day.

He put it out of his mind instantly. He'd played solidly, he'd made some good tackles and he'd done his best to get some good moves going, but nothing had really worked. They'd done their best, but they'd still lost to a soft goal.

So that was it: he had played his last game.

Coach was standing outside the dressing room talking to a man in a long raincoat. The two of them looked up as Andy approached.

'Andy,' said Coach. 'This is Paul Mitchell. He's on the coaching staff at Borough.'

Andy recognized the name. Mitchell had been a defender for Borough a few years ago, but he'd never really made it.

Now Mitchell held out a hand for Andy to shake. 'I enjoyed the game,' he said. 'But that ref needs his eyes testing, doesn't he? You were never offside: you timed that run just right.'

And just then Andy started to realize that maybe he

44

did have something – something that this Paul Mitchell had been looking for.

If only they would give him a chance.

Coach looked over Andy's shoulder. Someone else was joining them.

Andy turned and saw his father limping through the crowd, Grandad just behind him. The two of them came to stand by Andy without saying a word.

The scout from Borough looked at him oddly. 'Don't I know you?' he said. 'Didn't you used to play for—?'

Andy's father shook his head. 'That's all history,' he said. Then he put a hand on Andy's shoulder, and added, 'But this is the lad with the future. We should be talking about *him*, right? He's my son. With a bit of help from an ex-pro he could turn into something really special, couldn't he? What do you say? Do you want to talk about it?'

The scout nodded. 'Yes,' he said. 'Yes, I think I do.'

WILL SOMEONE, SOMEWHERE, PLEASE PLAY US AT FOOTBALL?

by David Ross

'It's not our fault.'

'We couldn't help it.'

'Doesn't matter whose fault it is. We've still got no-one to play against.'

Sarvindar Patel, Vernon Cramb and Gary Sandford were discussing the problem as they walked home from Skimpole Street School. Sarvindar was the captain of Skimpole Street's first and only soccer eleven. Vernon was a defender. Gary was the team's best striker and his mum was their trainer. Not many school teams had someone's mum for a trainer, but Skimpole Street School had its own way of doing things. Also, no-one but Mrs Sandford was willing to take on the job.

The problem was a serious one. They had a football

team, but no-one wanted to play against them. A short time before, Skimpole Street had been thrown out of the Inter-School Football Competition. This was the result of a totally disastrous game against Stapleton Road School. It had gone wrong from the start. The Brown twins had started fighting on the pitch. A large dog belonging to a Skimpole Streeter's uncle had come on to the field and bitten a hole in the referee's shorts. Gary Sandford's mother had tried to join the side as a substitute and had been sent off by the referee. Sarvindar had missed a penalty. And, the worst thing of all, Bayram Abdullah's father had put something in the half-time samosas. He wanted to give the Stapleton Road side a belly-ache. But the samosas got mixed up and there were belly-aches all round. And the biggest belly-ache of all was the referee's. At half-time the score was 22–0. There never was a second half, because of the samosas.

As a result, Skimpole Street was well and truly out of the Inter-school League. And whenever Mr Watkins, the headmaster, tried to ring up neighbouring schools or boys' clubs to arrange a friendly game, the answer was always the same sort of thing: 'Oh, I'm afraid we're booked up for the rest of the term . . .' 'Sorry, we don't seem to have a slot . . .' And even: 'No, thanks very much – we don't want to get mixed up with you lot.'

It was all very depressing. Even Mr Watkins, who prided himself on his Positive Thinking, could not come up with any ideas.

47

'What's the use of having a football team when no-one will play us?' muttered Sarvindar.

Gary shrugged his shoulders and sighed. There didn't seem to be any answer to that.

Training was after school on Tuesdays. Usually about fifteen boys were there, keen and ready to start. But on the next training day only three members of the team turned up to greet their trainer – Gary Sandford, Sarvindar Patel and Bayram Abdullah.

'What's going on?' asked Mrs Carrie Sandford. 'Where's everybody? Have they forgotten what day it is? Has plague broken out?'

Sarvindar looked embarrassed. 'I think it's because we don't have anyone to play against,' he said. 'They don't see any point in coming to train.'

'Oh, don't they? I'll soon put that right,' said Carrie Sandford. 'If I take the trouble to be trainer, I expect the side to turn out – tell them that I expect to see everyone next week, or else. We need to keep the team in shape. After all, we don't want to lose, if we do get a fixture.'

'But we've still got no-one to play against,' pointed out Sarvindar.

'Well, I've got an idea about that,' she said.

'What is it, Mum?' asked Gary.

'You'll just have to wait to find out. I have to consult first.'

And she would say no more.

'Sarvindar,' said Gary Sandford quietly, a few days

later, 'you remember my mum said she had an idea about who we could play football against?'

'Yes, I remember.'

'Well, she told me what it was.'

'What was it?'

'We're going to play the PTA ladies' team.'

'WHAT?' Sarvindar Patel's eyes went as round as marbles.

'The PTA ladies' team,' repeated Gary.

'What's that?'

'It's people's mums, basically.'

'I didn't know there was a PTA ladies' team.'

'There wasn't. But there is one now. My mum's just started it.'

'Are you serious?'

'She is. Why not? She says she's got a full side and they're very keen. It's good for keeping fit. And she says it's to raise money for the school as well. They hope a lot of people will pay to come and watch.'

'But—' Sarvindar spluttered. 'People's mothers!' The whole idea seemed too wild to be possible.

Gary, having got over his own surprise, was being ultra-cool. 'Yeah, people's mothers. So what?'

'What will the others say?'

'I don't know. We can tell them it's OK. I mean, we'd be bound to win. How many mothers can play football?'

'I suppose we would.' Sarvindar looked doubtful. 'Who's in it – the mothers' team?'

'There's my mum, of course. Vernon's, Piano Legs's, a few others who haven't got sons in the school team. Oh, and Mrs Brown.'

'Norman and Kevin's mum?' Sarvindar suddenly looked alarmed.

'Yeah, Mrs Brown.' Gary looked thoughtful, despite his efforts to keep a cool air. If the Brown twins were a bit of a handful at times, then their mother was something else. Mrs Brown was famous for several things, including her large size, her heavy hand, her loud voice, and her tendency to say the kind of things that most people left unsaid, or didn't even think.

'Imagine bumping into Mrs Brown at full speed.'

'No thanks, I'd rather not. But she's in goal, I think.'

'That means Piano Legs is safe, but no-one else.'

Piano Legs Cooper was the Skimpole Street keeper, a safe pair of hands. He had been off sick at the time of you-know-what, or the result might have been different.

When the news was broken to them, and they had got over their shock, some of the team thought it was quite a good idea. Others were not so sure. The ones to be truly horrified were Norman and Kevin Brown. For once they agreed with each other.

'Play against our mum?' said Norman. 'Are you kidding? We'd get a thick ear if we took the ball off her.'

'I'm not playing if she's playing,' said Kevin. He folded his arms, and stuck out his chin. 'No way.'

But on the day, they were in the team.

'She said we had to play. Or else,' Kevin said.

The referee was Mr Gareth Watkins, headmaster of Skimpole Street School. He had tried to avoid the job, but Mrs Sandford had persuaded him.

'I'm not very good at refereeing,' he protested.

'Don't worry, Mr Watkins. I'll help you,' said Carrie.

Now the moment had come. He stood clutching his whistle, and looking unhappy. A large and cheerful crowd of parents and pupils had come to Willoughby Park to watch the game. The local newspaper had even sent along a photographer. Mrs Sandford was pleased to spot the secretary of the local youth league in the crowd. Surely we'll get some games after this, she thought. Everyone clapped and cheered noisily as the two teams ran on. Both sides were wearing the green shirts and yellow shorts of the Skimpole Street School strip, but it was not hard to tell them apart.

'Come on, mums!'

'Come on, boys!'

Gary Sandford found himself facing his mother at the kick-off. She grinned fiercely at him. Then the whistle went, and suddenly she was gone. So was the ball. He turned to see her moving down the field, easily evading the defenders. She clipped the ball across to Mrs Wong, a slender lady who could run at terrific speed. Mrs Wong, realizing she was offside, passed the ball across to Mrs Metcalf, a rather absent-minded lady who had just joined the team and had had only one practice session. Mrs Metcalf looked at the ball as though it were about to explode at her feet, and then kicked it in the wrong direction. It rolled gently back upfield, where Vernon Cramb ran to get possession and sent it zinging across to the midfielders.

'We're playing that way, Mrs Metcalf,' cried Carrie, pointing to Piano Legs, crouching in his goalmouth.

Carrie, as the boys' trainer, had taught them to tackle closely. But very soon she found that they were not tackling as closely as they usually did. It was easy for the ladies to keep possession. After only five minutes Carrie came storming to the ten-yard line with the ball, and Vernon, instead of tackling, stood respectfully aside. The other defenders hung back.

'Oi!' shouted Sarvindar. 'Do something.'

But it was too late. Carrie sent the ball high into the net and ran back in triumph. Soon after that, Mrs Cramb broke through a feeble defence and scored a second goal.

Mothers 2, boys 0.

'Tackle, can't you!' shouted Carrie to the boys.

'Tackle!' called Sarvindar Patel to his team. 'Get the ball!' But whenever he himself came up against one of the ladies, he suddenly felt shy, and didn't push the tackle, and off she went with the ball.

The mums were winning – and winning easily.

Mrs Brown had been placed in goal. Norman and Kevin, usually keen to play forward, kept well away from her. To Sarvindar it looked almost as if she could touch both posts by stretching out her arms. Late in the first half, when the ball came racing to his boot after a neat midfield pass from Gary, he tried a long shot from his favourite position out on the right-hand side. He gave it all he had, and it went in swift and low, but Mrs Brown stooped, gathered it up easily, and hurled it back into the field with a bark of laughter. Mrs Cramb took it, dodged round Bayram, and was off for goal again. The backs gathered hesitantly. Mrs Cramb, showing skill that amazed her son Vernon, nutmegged the ball through, and transferred the ball to Mrs Wong, who shot for goal. As the ball streaked in towards the top of the net, Piano Legs made a heroic leap and pushed it off to one side. Charlie Gibson, the tallest boy in the team, tried to head it away, missed, and it rolled for a corner. Mrs Sandford took the kick, and sent it to Mrs Cramb. Vernon, desperate to show his father and sisters, who were all watching, that he was not going to be outplayed by his mother, darted in to intercept, and got the ball away.

At half-time the score was still 2–0. Each side had a serious talk in their separate halves of the pavilion.

'We've got to do something,' said Sarvindar Patel. 'Otherwise we'll be known for ever as the team that was beaten by their mothers. It would be even worse than you–know–what.'

'It's amazing,' said Charlie Gibson. 'They can actually play, some of them.'

'Yeah, well, what do we do?' said Norman.

'We're being too nice,' said Sarvindar. 'Remember what Mrs Sandford always says to us: "The reason for playing is to win." We're not playing to win. We're letting them walk away with the ball. We have to get possession, keep possession, and go for the goal. Keep the ball high. They're not so good with it in the air. Boys can jump better than ladies. If we can keep it high, and head it, we might have a chance. Charlie should stay up just inside their half, and be ready to head the ball on to where Gary or I or Bayram can try for goal. OK? It's our best chance.'

Meanwhile, on the other side of the partition Carrie Sandford was saying: 'What do we do? If we seem to hold back, they'll be insulted. They'll think we've let them win. But if we do win, they'll be terribly upset. Oh dear, maybe this match wasn't such a good idea.'

'Well, I'm certainly not going to let them win, if I can help it,' said Mrs Brown stoutly. 'Norman and Kevin will never let me hear the end of it.'

'After all,' said Mrs Wong, 'we are a team too. We should play to win. That's what you told us.'

'All right, ladies,' said Carrie. She flung her hands up in the air. 'Let the best team win. After all, I've trained both. I can't complain about the result, whatever it is.'

Mr Gareth Watkins was not having a good time. He was not used to running about, and it was quite difficult to watch where the ball was going. Quite often, he found himself on top of the ball, in the middle of a little group of players, and had to skip quickly out of the way.

Mrs Sandford tried to help him by hissing, 'Throw-in', or 'Corner'. Once she said 'Dead ball' to him, and he was completely baffled. There were a few mocking noises from the crowd, and Mrs Brown said something that sounded like 'What a prat.' But he could not simply follow Mrs Sandford round the field. The second half seemed to stretch endlessly ahead of him.

The mums immediately noticed the difference in the boys' play in the second half. The ball was always rising into the air, and members of the first eleven were leaping up to head it, or racing ahead to trap it and play it on. Once they almost scored. After a long header from Charlie, and a break down the right from Gary, who crossed the ball to Kevin, Kevin had the ball at the ten-yard line, with only his mother to beat. He took a deep breath and prepared for a mighty kick.

'Don't you dare, Kevin Brown,' she bellowed, just as he was about to let fly. The ball went hopelessly wide and Kevin fled away, his mother's laughter ringing out behind him.

'Come on, Gary Sandford, do something,' called Gary's mother, seeing him standing in midfield.

'I am doing something,' he muttered.

Still 2–0. But Sarvindar's tactics were having some effect. The boys were now playing to keep the ball under their control. Vernon had sent a cross over to Bayram, which Mrs Wong had intercepted. Catching his mother's eye, Gary dashed off towards her and she kicked it high towards the left wing. Charlie rose up like a sea-lion from its pool and headed it back to Gary, who passed it to Bayram, who dummied it past Mrs Wong and sent it streaking under Mrs Brown's arm into the net. That was not all. After a throw-in Sarvindar took the ball, then lost it to Mrs Cramb, who found herself blocked by Bayram and sent the ball to Mrs Metcalf.

'Oh dear,' said Mrs Metcalf. 'Which way are we playing?'

'This way!' cried Carrie, but it was too late.

As Mrs Metcalf stood wondering, Sarvindar sneakily tapped the ball away from her and set off with it at a run. Mothers loomed up but he dodged them. He heard his teammates shouting 'To me!' but he kept the ball until the last minute, and then, as Mrs Brown seemed to fill all the space in front of him, he swiftly slid the ball across to Gary, who had paced him all the way down and now moved into position. In his excitement, Gary almost missed the kick. The ball seemed to wobble off his boot with painful slowness, and stopped just over the line, where Mrs Brown fell on top of it like a vast collapsing jelly. It was 2–2.

The crowd on the sidelines were hopping up and down, and cheering. Both teams had now forgotten everything but the desire to win. Mr Watkins had never been so active. The ball was sent racing about the pitch, with players in frantic chase. The midfield action was intense. But for a long time there were no more goals. There was a narrow squeak at the boys' end when

Carrie and Mrs Cooper arrived with the ball, pursued by half a dozen Skimpole Streeters. Piano Legs stood watching his mother's skill with amazement, until he suddenly remembered he was supposed to be keeping goal. Mrs Cooper aimed for his left. Piano Legs prepared to dive, then saw the glint in his mother's eye. With a flash of inspiration, he dived to the right, just as she smacked the ball that way with her left boot. With his fingertips he just managed to push it clear. Mothers were crowding round the goal for the corner, but a Skimpole back shunted the ball to him, and he sent it up and away with a lofty kick, and the play stampeded off into the mothers' half.

It was very near to full time. The boys were jostling close to the mums' goalmouth, when the incident happened. Mr Watkins, constantly looking this way and that as the ball was moved around, felt as though his head would come loose.

'Oi, mind out, ref,' called Mrs Brown, as he jumped across in front of her. 'He's always getting in the way, that windbag,' she added.

Then, for a moment, Norman Brown had the ball, and hastily punted it across to Bayram with the side of his boot. Mrs Wong and Bayram got to it at the same time, with a crowd of others close by. Their boots struck it together. It shot off violently, and bounced hard against Mr Watkins's bottom just as he was turning round to watch where it was going.

'Ouch!' cried Mr Watkins. The ball, deflected, but

still travelling at speed, passed through a gap between several players and, to everyone's astonishment, flopped over inside the goalmouth.

'Goal!' shouted Sarvindar.

'No-ball!' shouted Mrs Sandford.

Both of them looked appealingly at Mr Watkins, who was rubbing his behind.

'Er,' he said.

'Come on, ref,' called Mrs Brown. 'It was a no-ball, wasn't it?'

'I kicked it,' said Bayram. 'He just got in the way.'

'Hold on, *I* kicked it,' said Mrs Wong.

Everyone looked at Mr Watkins.

'Even if Mrs Wong kicked it, it would be an own-goal,' said Sarvindar. 'The ball crossed the line. That means it's a goal. Doesn't it, sir?'

'Er, I don't know,' said Mr Watkins. He looked around despairingly. 'Does anyone know what the rules say?'

No-one answered.

'Perhaps we should have a drop-in,' said Mrs Sandford.

'A drop-in?' asked Mr Watkins, who was beginning to hate mothers, boys and football. His legs were tired, his bottom was sore, and he didn't know what to do.

'Yes, you drop the ball down on the spot where the incident happened, and play goes on from there.'

'But we've got a goal,' protested Sarvindar Patel. 'It wouldn't be fair.'

'What a hopeless ref,' murmured Mrs Brown, rather too loudly. 'Make up your mind.'

Mr Watkins went quite red. His cheeks puffed out until he looked like a big, bad-tempered baby. For a long moment, he said nothing. Then, at last, he had a Positive Thought. He looked at his watch and said: 'It's time.' He blew a long, shrill blast on his whistle.

'The game is over,' he announced. 'The score is two all, plus one to the referee. That's two–two–one. It may be unusual, I'm not saying it's quite the normal thing, but that's my decision.'

'It's unheard of,' said Mrs Brown.

'I don't mind,' said Mrs Sandford.

'I don't mind,' said Sarvindar Patel.

Solemnly, the two captains shook hands with each other, while the photographer crouched to snap them.

Then Mrs Sandford suddenly burst out laughing. 'After all, this is Skimpole Street School,' she said. 'Anything can happen here.'

DON'T TELL ME!
by David Belbin

Dad had promised that he'd do his best. But getting tickets wasn't easy. You couldn't just go to the ground and buy two. Most of the seats went to season ticket holders. Chris didn't have a season ticket. You had to know somebody who knew someone. You had to be prepared to pay over the odds. Chris tried not to get too excited. Even Dad's best might not be good enough.

It was Chris's birthday. There were plenty of presents waiting downstairs. Not one looked like match tickets. Trying not to look worried, she began opening them. The Subbuteo set was dead good. So was the new Liverpool FC scarf. Next came a book of football stories. Chris opened it. Maybe a pair of tickets would fall out . . .

No joy.

Dad saw what Chris was thinking. 'Sorry,' he told her. 'I spent ages on the phone. I asked around in the pub. But tickets are like gold dust this year.'

Chris knew why the tickets were so hard to get. Tomorrow wasn't just any old match. It was the big derby at Goodison. In other words, Liverpool were playing Everton, away. Not only that, but Everton and Liverpool were both close to the top of the table. For once, the result really mattered.

'We'll get tickets when they're playing at Anfield,' Dad said. 'Promise.'

'Thanks,' Chris told him. 'Don't worry. It's all right.'

Later on, Dan came round. He'd brought Chris a signed photo of Michael Owen.

Chris was ecstatic. 'How did you get it?'

'I wrote off ages ago. I was getting worried. It only came yesterday.'

'It's brilliant. I'll get it framed.'

'And we'll be seeing him play tomorrow.'

Chris's face fell.

'Your dad did get tickets, didn't he?'

Chris gave a sad shake of the head.

'I'm really sorry,' Dan said. 'Dad's taking Tim and me.'

'No worries,' Chris lied.

It wasn't fair. Dan's brother Tim wasn't a big football fan. He was mad about swimming. He trained obsessively for tournaments. Going to the match would

63

mean nothing to Tim. Whereas, to Chris, it meant everything. But Tim didn't like Chris. There was no way that he would give up his match ticket.

They played with Chris's new Subbuteo team. Dan was Everton, while Chris had Liverpool. They rehearsed the next day's game, playing ten minutes a half, but Chris's heart wasn't in it. Dan won, 3–1.

'Want to come over and play on my computer?' Dan asked.

Chris said yes. Dan only lived across the road. It was a grey, rainy day. Despite this, Dan's brother Tim was outside, having a kick-about with some mates.

'Eh up, sprog!' he said to Chris. 'How's my brother's girlfriend?'

'Get lost!' Chris said.

'Ooh, you're touchy today, Christina! Got a ticket for the match tomorrow?'

Chris shook her head.

'Too bad,' Tim said.

'Come on,' Dan said. 'Let's go inside.'

They went up to Dan's room.

'Sorry,' Dan said. 'I'd rather go to the match with you. It was great on my birthday.'

Chris wished he hadn't reminded her of that. Going to the match against Spurs had been Dan's last birthday treat.

'Forget it,' she told Dan. 'Let's talk about something else.'

★   ★   ★

At her birthday dinner that night Chris was very quiet.

'What's wrong?' Dad asked.

Chris didn't want to mention missing the game. 'Just Tim, teasing me,' she said.

'Boys are nitwits at that age,' Mum said. 'They don't mean anything. I'll bet that in a few years' time he'll be trying to work up the courage to ask you out.'

'Don't tell me that!' Chris said, pretending to be sick. 'Ugh!'

Going out with Tim Naylor was the most horrible thought in the world. Chris had seen what effect having boyfriends had on girls who used to go to her school. They went all soppy. They grew their hair. And most of them lost all interest in football. Chris had no intention of letting that happen to her.

'Can I stay up to watch *Match of the Day* tomorrow?' Chris asked.

'What time's it on?' Mum wanted to know.

'Ten forty-five,' Chris said, in a small voice.

'That's way past your bed-time, young lady.' Her parents were very strict about bed-times.

'But it's my birthday weekend,' Chris moaned. 'And I need to see the match, even if it's just the highlights.'

'I'll tape it for you,' Dad said. 'You can watch it in the morning.'

'That's *not the same*!' Chris protested.

'Why not?' Dad asked. 'You'll know the result anyway.'

'No, I won't,' Chris told him. 'I'll avoid finding out.'

'How will you do that?' Mum asked.

'Simple. I won't watch the telly, or look at teletext, or listen to the radio.'

'Or look out of the window at half five when all the supporters are coming back from the match?' Dad added. 'Or answer the phone? We're surrounded by people who support Everton or Liverpool. It's very hard to avoid finding out the score when you live round here.'

'I'll manage it, if you let me stay up,' Chris promised.

'You'll never manage to stay awake that late,' Dad said jokily.

Chris liked her sleep, it was true. She could fall asleep anywhere, any time.

'Bet you I will,' Chris told him.

'We'll see.'

Chris hated it when Dad said 'We'll see'. It meant he hoped that she'd have forgotten about whatever it was before he and Mum made up their minds.

'That's not good enough,' she told him pushily. 'It's not a school day. You haven't got a leg to stand on.'

'Oh, all right. It is your birthday. If you can stay awake, you can watch the highlights with me.'

'And you won't tell me the score?'

'No,' Dad said. 'In fact, I thought I'd avoid finding out myself. That way, we can both enjoy the suspense.'

The following afternoon Chris's Auntie Fran and Uncle Richard were coming over for lunch, bringing presents. Her uncle and aunt were late, as usual. It was a longish drive from Sheffield. Chris watched from the window. At one thirty she saw Dan, Tim and their dad setting off for the match. Dan cast a sad glance in her direction. Chris ducked out of sight. She didn't want him to feel guilty.

Richard and Fran showed up five minutes later, bearing presents.

'She looks just like me at her age, doesn't she, sis?' Auntie Fran said.

Mum agreed.

'You know, Chris, until I was fourteen I used to get everyone to call me Frank. Didn't I, sis?'

Mum nodded.

'What happened when you were fourteen?' Chris wanted to know, but Auntie Fran was already talking about something else.

'It's a pity you couldn't be at the match today,' Uncle Richard said.

Chris, frustrated, didn't reply.

'What's wrong?' her uncle asked.

As Dad explained, Chris ran upstairs to her room. Outside, dark clouds filled the sky, mirroring her misery. Chris hoped that everybody at the game got wet.

Lunch was a big affair, with roast beef, Yorkshire puddings and loads of vegetables. The conversation shifted from jobs to films to music to football.

'It's nearly three forty-five,' Uncle Richard said, as

they finished their dessert. 'Can I put on Radio Five for the half-time reports?'

'No!' Chris yelled.

'Christina, don't be so rude,' Mum said.

Dad explained about the pact they'd made.

'You'll never manage it,' Auntie Fran said. 'There's always someone who'll spoil things.'

'Have you got a radio in the other room?' Uncle Richard asked.

'It's broken,' Dad said, and looked at Chris.

She wasn't going to tell her uncle that she had a radio in her bedroom. Suppose he gave the score away?

'I'll just go out to the car and listen in there,' Uncle Richard said. But as he got to the door, the rain finally started. It was a huge downpour. 'Maybe I'll wait and find out on the way home,' he said.

After lunch, Chris went up to her room and played World Cup '98 on her computer. She'd played the full simulation a hundred times. Nevertheless, she'd never managed to get the ideal result. This would be England beating France in extra time with Michael Owen scoring the winning goal. Doing the simulation, Chris lost track of time. As she steered the team into the semi-finals she heard a car pulling in across the road. Mr Naylor sounded the horn. They were back from the match.

Angry, Chris stopped herself from going to the window. One glance at Dan's face and she'd know the result. She was going to her own match, on the telly, tonight.

A bit later Mum yelled to her, 'Your uncle and aunt are going! Come and say goodbye.'

Chris went down and said her farewells.

'Hope your team won,' Uncle Richard said.

Chris thanked them again for her present, a T-shirt. When they were gone, she looked at her watch. It was nearly time for *Xena: Warrior Princess*. 'Can I have the telly on, Mum?'

It was Dad who replied. 'All right, but I just want to get the news headlines first.' He switched the set on, then began flicking channels. Chris half-watched a cartoon, a game show, some ancient film, adverts, then the news.

'And now over to Nigel Winterbottom for the sport . . .'

'No!' Chris screamed.

'All right, all right,' Dad said, and switched to Chris's programme.

Grandma popped in just after it was over. Grandma Tate was always telling Dad off for spoiling Chris. Chris didn't like her as much as her other grandma, who lived in Sheffield. This was partly because she was strict, but mainly because she was a Manchester United supporter.

'Pity about the football,' was the first thing she said, after Chris had kissed her 'hello'.

'Don't tell me!' Chris yelled. '*Don't tell me!*'

'What on earth . . . ?'

Dad explained about the pact that they'd made not to find out the result.

'I see,' Grandma Tate said. 'Well, if that's how you feel, I certainly won't say another word on the subject. In fact, wild horses would not drag what happened out of me.'

'Thank you,' Dad said.

'You won't be thanking me when you do find out,' Grandma said.

What did she mean? Chris spent the next half-hour puzzling over it. 'Pity about the football.' Was it a pity because Liverpool had lost? Or was she being sarcastic? (Grandma Tate had a funny sense of humour.) Perhaps she meant that it was a pity from Dad and Chris's point of view. Then she'd said, 'You won't be thanking me when you do find out.' Chris didn't want to know what that meant. But she couldn't help thinking about it.

The phone rang. Chris was nearest, so she answered it. The voice on the other end was Dan's.

'I'd have thought you'd have been round by now,' her friend said.

'I don't want to know the result,' Chris told him. 'Dad and I are going to watch Match of the Day together later. So please don't spoil it.'

'Listen,' Dan said. 'I think—'

'Don't say another word,' Chris told him. 'I'll be able to tell what happened from the tone of your voice. You can tell me all about it tomorrow. I've got to go now. Bye.' She hung up.

A moment later the phone rang again. Chris answered.

It was her Uncle Paul, calling from Leeds. 'What about the match, then?' he asked.

Chris screamed, then hung up.

'What was all that about?' Mum asked a minute later. 'Who was on the phone?'

'Just Dan,' Chris fibbed. 'He wanted to tell me what happened in the match. That was why I screamed, so I couldn't hear him.'

'That's not like Dan,' Mum said. 'He's normally such a nice lad. Oh, look. I do believe he's coming over.'

Chris looked out of the window. There was Dan, sauntering over with a silly smile on his face. 'No!' Chris said. 'I won't see him.' She ran upstairs.

'I'm sorry, Dan,' Chris heard Mum saying before she slammed her bedroom door shut. Why did her best friend have to spoil it for her?

A moment later, Dad came in. 'What's wrong?' he asked. 'Why are you crying?'

Chris told him.

'I'm really sorry I couldn't get the tickets,' Dad said. 'You have to believe that I tried my hardest.'

'I do believe you,' Chris told him. 'It's Dan I'm upset with. He knew how much I wanted to go to the match. He could have waited before trying to tell me the result.'

'I'm sure you'll make it up,' Dad said. 'Now, believe me. Nobody is going to tell us the score.'

'Good,' Chris said.

She and Dad went downstairs. She hoped that he and

Mum wouldn't notice that she'd left the phone off the hook.

'Did Dan tell you about the match?' Dad asked Mum in the kitchen.

'He did,' Mum said, with the suggestion of a smile.

'Then don't say a single word. Not a hint. Neither of us want to know. Understood?'

Mum shrugged. 'Understood.'

Chris joined Mum and Dad watching *Blind Date*, then the film, which was boring. By the end she was starting to doze off. The news came on. Chris went upstairs to change into her pyjamas. Then, when no-one was looking, she put the phone back on the hook. Nobody ever called this late. When she came back down, the news was still on.

'Suppose they tell us the results?' she said.

'Don't worry,' Dad said. 'It's the same channel as *Match of the Day*. If they're going to reveal the results, they always warn you.'

Chris was both excited and tired. How could being excited make you tired?

'Listen,' she said to Mum and Dad. 'If I fall asleep, you've got to wake me when the match comes on. Promise?'

'We promise,' Mum said.

Chris closed her eyes. Nothing could go wrong now. It was too late for anyone to come round. She and Dad had managed to avoid the result. Now she could really enjoy the highlights.

* * *

When Chris woke, it was morning, and she was in her own bed. She tried to remember the match. Who had won? She had dreamt of a Robbie Fowler hat trick, but that was only a dream. Wasn't it? Chris snapped awake and realized, with horror, what had happened. Mum and Dad must have put her to bed. They had let her miss the match!

Chris nearly exploded. She wanted to be fair. Maybe Mum and Dad had tried to wake her, but failed. Perhaps she'd been in such a deep sleep that . . . but no. It made no sense. She looked at her watch. Not yet seven. Mum and Dad would sleep for another hour. Still, they must have videoed the game for her.

Chris tried to convince herself that seeing the video would be good enough. After all, if the game wasn't live, what did it matter when you watched it – as long as you didn't know the result? Chris got dressed and went downstairs to the living room.

She tried every tape piled up by the TV. No *Match of the Day*. Chris couldn't believe it. How could they not have taped it for her? Call themselves parents? She hated them!

Then she heard the familiar sound of a squeaky bicycle. Tim Naylor, Dan's brother, did a morning paper round. At last, at last, she'd be able to find out the result! Chris hurried to the door, and waited for the paper to come through the letterbox. She saw Tim's silhouette as he reached forward to put it in.

73

'Chris? Is that you?' he asked gently.

'Y-yes.'

'What are you doing, waiting for the paper?'

'I – I . . .' Oh, what did it matter? She'd missed the match. She might as well let Tim tell her. 'I want to know what the score was yesterday,' she said.

'You mean nobody's told you yet? I thought Dan came round.'

'I wouldn't see him. I didn't want to know the score.'

Suddenly, Tim began to laugh. 'I'm off,' he said when he stopped.

'Wait,' Chris called out. 'The paper . . .'

'I'm not letting you read about it,' Tim told her. 'I'm getting Dan.'

Frustrated, Chris curled herself up in a corner of the hall, waiting for her friend. She knew that she could go and turn on the telly, look up the result on Teletext. But she might as well wait. If telling her meant so much to Dan, let him tell her. Though why he had to rub it in, she didn't know.

There was a faint knock on the door. Chris answered it. There was Dan, wearing his track suit.

'Fancy a quick kick-about before breakfast?' he said.

'All right,' she told him.

Dan threw the newspaper onto the hall floor and Chris followed him outside. He'd got a new leather ball for Christmas.

'How was the match?' she asked, unable to hold back any longer.

'Rubbish,' he said. 'It was grey and horrible and the pitch was wet. Both sides looked really uncomfortable.'

'Yes, but what was the result?' Chris asked.

'You really don't know, do you?'

'Know what?' Chris demanded, impatiently.

'There wasn't a result!' Dan told her.

'What do you mean, *there wasn't a result*?'

'There was a big downpour at half-time when the score was nil–nil. Then the floodlights failed.'

'So?'

'They spent ages trying to fix them but each time they came back on, they went off again within a minute. It was dead frustrating.'

'What happened in the end?' Chris asked impatiently.

'The game was abandoned.'

'I see,' Chris said, flabbergasted. No wonder Mum and Dad hadn't woken her up. That must have been what Grandma and Uncle Paul wanted to tell her. And she'd been so rude to them.

'You haven't heard the best bit yet,' Dan said.

'Tell me!' Chris demanded.

Two and a half weeks later Chris, Dan and his dad sat in the Gladys Road end, which was the away supporters section at Goodison Park. All three of them were yelling their loudest: 'Come on! Come on! Pass the ball, can't you!'

Robbie Fowler dummied one of the Everton defenders, then made a pass, looking for Jamie

Redknapp. The ball was intercepted by the goalie, but he couldn't hold onto it. Paul Ince had a shot and hit the bar. Suddenly, from nowhere, Michael Owen dived in for a header.

'G-O-A-L!!!!'

All three of them hugged each other. The half-time whistle blew.

'It's a pity your Tim couldn't be here,' Chris said, with a smile to show that she wasn't serious.

'Tim couldn't miss the swimming tournament,' his dad said. 'It's much more important to him. The footie's on telly later, so I'll video him the highlights. He can watch them tomorrow.'

'But he'll know the result by then,' Chris pointed out.

'Doesn't really matter, does it?' Dan said. 'If you're not there, it's never the same.'

And all three of them agreed that it wasn't.

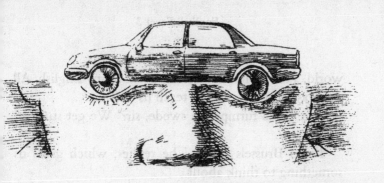

ERIK'S ANGELS
by Jonathan Kebbe

Up at six – wash in cold water – run round the frosty
field – forty press-ups – breakfast – fight over the last
piece of toast – make your bed – sweep the floor –
polish your shoes – 'I want to see my face in those shoes,
Dekko!' – then a long morning of boring lessons –
'Capital of Russia? capital of Turkey? capital of
England, Dekko?' – 'Liverpool, sir' – 'Go and stand in
the corner!' – Then lunch, which is always puky – arts
and crafts, cross-country or a bruising gym period, and
a poxy supper and a bit of free time, and always – 'Keep
the noise down! Come here, boy! Empty your pockets!
Go and stand outside Mr Sikes's office . . .'

I hate this place. Hilljoy House it's called. We call it
Helljoy.

Then the other day Mr Eriksonn comes into our

world, a tall blond bloke who speaks funny English. All the way from Sweden to teach us – *drama!*

'Are you a turnip or a swede, sir?' We get stuck in right away.

'I'm a Brussels sprout,' he replies, which gives us something to think about.

The drama's great, but Mr Sikes – Psycho, we call him – stops it 'cos we get over-excited. So Brussels Sprout asks can he run a football team?

'No no no, Mr Eriksonn! I've told you, these boys are hooligans, they'd kill each other.'

So Brussels Sprout says: 'I've made enquiries, and there will be soon a five-a-side tournament in the parish. What about a hand-picked team to represent Hilljoy?'

Mr Sikes laughs so hard, he has to sit down.

'Please, Mr Sikes, let me try.'

'Let me try! let me try!' we sing while Eriksonn gives us all a trial and says, 'You want to play for the school?' and we say 'Yes, sure!' and laugh some more.

When the training starts, we stop laughing. 'Take it easy, sir, slow down, this is bad for our image,' and off we slope to the jacks for a smoke.

Then old Erik gets mad for the first time. 'You can swear at me, you can throw chalk at me – I don't mind, but I *do* mind to see you throw your lives away. You're good boys underneath, and you have to believe in yourselves.'

We go all tingly. We're not used to being called

good. 'Don't be a sap, sir,' I say, 'we're bad, that's why we're here.'

We give the training another go. Erik makes it more fun this time, tells us to *express ourselves*. We run around jinking and flicking the ball and doing little ballet steps – tra-la-la! – expressing ourselves! Then he announces a friendly match against the nearest school in the area – Gretton College Prep School.

We split our sides. 'Good joke, sir.' We see he's serious and we're nearly sick.

'You have plenty in common with Gretton. It costs a fortune to send them there, and it costs a fortune to keep you here. Also it's a boarding school – a prison – like here!'

'But they're posh, sir – what'll we say to them?'

'You're going to a football match, Declan, not a dance.'

Now the training really starts. We've something to focus on – the snots of Gretton. Let me introduce you to the team. I'm Dekko, captain – half-Irish, half-mad and a bit fat and lazy, but a cool midfield general, stroking the ball about while the others do the huffing and puffing. I'm not a nice person to know if you drive a car. I hate cars. I kick dents in them or scratch them with coins or bottle tops. My mum was knocked flying by a hit-and-run driver. She's been in a home ever since, mumbling and dribbling and wondering what's going on. Last time I visited she screams: 'Help! Thief! Get him away from me!' Just seeing a car go by makes my blood boil. Psycho has to employ an old man all day to guard the teachers' cars. The magistrate says (posh voice), 'If you promise not to attack any more cars I'll think about releasing you.' I say: 'Yes sir, I promise sir,' and a month later they send me home to Gran. Gran kisses me and makes my tea. Then I see the photo of Mum on the mantelpiece, all shiny and smiling, and I run onto the street and pick a smart new Renault and kick its lights in – *smash*, *crash*, fantastic feeling! I'm back here before the glass has settled. I lie awake thinking about the hit-and-run man. He could have stopped to help Mum. If I could get my hands on him . . .

In goal we've got Clubsy. He's a complete nutter, laughs all the time about nothing. We imitate him, the whole school – fifty-five boys – hobbling into class and falling about laughing. It makes the teachers really mad. Clubsy switches his hobble this way and that so we have to concentrate to copy him, and sometimes he gives a sudden mad twist, so when we try and follow we all fall over and *he* falls about laughing. He may be a wobbly walker, but between his posts he's a miracle of flight. Clubsy's in here 'cos he got sick of being bullied and stabbed two boys in the face. 'Every time they look in the mirror' – he laughs – 'they'll remember me.'

Then there's Smokes, who plays forward. He's got the worst stammer in the world. 'P-p-p-pass the b-b-butter, D-D-D-Dekko, you d-d-d-dunce!' But for some reason, with a ball at his feet, he speaks perfect: 'Quick! – pass it – call that a cross, you clown?' No-one talks about how he got here, but everyone knows things were very bad at home, and Smokes set fire to his school. They sent him to a special school and he set fire to that. We have to watch him, 'cos he gets really upset when a teacher shouts at him, and he could send us all to Heaven in a ball of smoke. He wears Gianfranco Zola on his shirt, but plays more like the Hunchback of Notre Dame.

Then there's Mally, our other striker. I was daft enough to call him 'Paki' when I came here, and he jabbed two fingers in my eyes so I couldn't see for a week. His home stuff was very bad too, but we don't talk about it. He's in here 'cos he went from breaking into cars and stealing radios to breaking into houses and stealing stereos – and he was only nine! Mally's a little wizard, a bag of tricks, a nightmare for defences.

Finally there's JB, who's black and doesn't say much and listens to music under his pillow. He came to Helljoy with the name JB, but refused to say what his initials were for – something weird, we guessed, like Jasper Barebottom, or Jammy Beggar. JB's got no parents – nobody quite knows what he did with them – and started shop-lifting at the age of four! – walking out with his shorts stuffed with sweets. We hid his CDs and threatened to pulp them till he confessed that JB stands for Jelly Beans. JB's tall and skinny and rises above defences like an ostrich. Sometimes.

The big day's come. We're wearing clean kit, we've brushed our teeth, we've talked tactics and we're all ready to thrash the nobs of Gretton. We pile into the clapped-out minibus – which I've scratched a thousand times with nails and coins.

'You boys be good for Mr Eriksonn,' says Psycho, 'and be on your best behaviour, right?'

We're on our best behaviour – till halfway to Gretton, when we get out our cigs and light up. The minibus fills with smoke. Erik goes: 'Who's smoking?'

'Sorry, sir, want one?' I say. 'Have one of mine.'

'Are you crazy? Before a match? It's the worst thing!'

'Oh sorry, sir, sorry sir' – we all madly pretend to put them out.

Then Jelly Beans says he feels sick. So Erik stops and JB jumps out. 'I feel sick too, sir,' goes Smokes, and jumps out. 'Me too, it must be the cigs, sir,' cries Clubsy, and jumps out. 'Me too,' goes Mally, 'Me too,' I say, and we're all out and running down the slope away from the road and back into the village, leaving poor old Erik with a bus and no team. I go into the sweetshop and distract the old geezer while the others grab the chocs and run. He goes: 'Are you with them?' I say: 'With them? You must be joking!' – and he runs out after them, while I select my favourite bars and stroll out.

Erik's so relieved to see us, he forgets to be angry: 'I thought you'd run away.'

'We wouldn't do that, sir – we just got some supplies in.'

'Are you crazy? Chocolate before a match? It's the worst thing!'

We just about make it to Gretton in the coughing spluttering minibus. We're all pumped up. We're going to make minced meat out of these snots. Driving through the gates our eyes nearly pop out. Gretton's like Buckingham Palace, the boys walk around in cloaks! The car park's full of BMWs and Range Rovers. My blood starts to boil. All that shiny steel just waiting for the sharpened edge of a 50p piece. And Smokes goes pale – all that ancient wood and stone waiting for the flame of his cigarette lighter. While Erik shakes hands with the enemy, Mally, Clubsy and Jelly Beans try and calm me and Smokes down. 'Let's destroy them, lads – in the gym.'

We meet the team. Blimey, they're huge! Ten-footers and they're only thirteen like us. We thought they'd be all airy-fairy and 'Hello there, chaps, how are you?' but they're worse, much worse, especially Jack, their smoothy captain – cold and sniffy like we're flea-bags. One of them's nice, Charlie, their goalie – or tries to be: 'Don't mind them, they're a bit nervous, they're not used to guys like you.' We have lunch in a massive dining room with a dome like a church, four hundred boys at forty long tables. That's about . . . . twelve to a table, isn't it? Everyone has a serviette, two knives, forks and spoons, and the tomato sauce comes in silver dishes. Someone bashes a gong and everyone stands for grace. *Amen.* They eat loudly and hungrily. Their manners are even worse than ours. We're too embarrassed to eat.

We get changed in silence. Erik tries to relax us: 'It's just a game, boys. I want you to enjoy it.'

'We'll kill them, sir.'

'No, no, you play your beautiful football like we practised.'

The gym's amazing, big enough for a gallery of spectators, a hundred faces curious to see the little criminals. We'll show them, snotty swines with their snotty parents and snotty money! 'Good luck, my brave boys' – Erik pats us on the back – 'express yourselves.'

And for a minute, that's what we do, neat little passes, quick one-twos, nice bit of magic from Mally, laser pass to Smokes and *wham!* – fierce shot smothered by Cheerful Charlie. Then they score on their first attack – the crowd roars! – and Smokes complains it was offside, which is thick. They're so big and strong they keep barging us off the ball. Mally gets knocked flying by Jack, their cocky captain, and we rush in and get booked – all five of us – for swearing. Cheers from the crowd! Then Clubsy brings down a man outside his box – penalty – more cheering – 2–0 – and Jelly Beans avenges Mally with a terrible tackle from behind on Jack the Ripper – the crowd boos! – and JB's sent off. At 5–0 Mally scores an in-off-the-post and celebrates with a rude sign to all their team – and gets sent off. More wild cheering. It's three of us now – a firebug, a car-vandal and a gammy leg against five fit giants. Smokes is so mad now he hacks a man down and accidentally treads on his face – and *he's* off. So there's

Clubsy in goal and me running round panting like a dog, and they score twice more in a minute and I explode: 'It's not fair!' and call the ref the biggest wally that ever walked the earth – and he sends *me* off. The crowds rolling around laughing. They've never seen anything like it. Clubsy's on his own. He takes off his gloves, gives a little bow and walks off.

We swagger out to the minibus, all-conquering heroes. Erik shakes hands sadly with the enemy and we drive off.

'Shut up, all of you!' shouts Erik. 'You've shamed yourselves.'

'B-b-b-but, sir,' says Smokes, 'we really sh-sh-sh-showed them!'

'Showed them what? Seven–one and the game stopped after only ten minutes! All our work for nothing. I don't care if you play good and lose seven–one. But that wasn't football, that was stupidity. Look at you all' – there's tears in his eyes – 'look at you! I'm leaving. I'm going home. What else can I do? I wanted to help you find your self-respect, but you're losers, every one of you.'

We do the rest of the journey in silence. We get ready for bed. I can't sleep. We're four to a dorm and I whisper: 'You awake, Mally?'

'Yep.'

'You really think he's going to leave?'

'I think so. If we don't do something.'

'Like what? Get him some flowers?'

Next day Psycho has us in and lines us up. Jesus gazes down from the wall over a poster saying: IN GOD WE TRUST. 'I've received a very serious complaint from the headmaster of Gretton.' Psycho's blue with rage. 'You're a disgrace to the school, a disgrace to yourselves, a disgrace to your parents' (some of us haven't got parents, sir). 'After all I and my staff have done for you. There's nothing left for me but to pray very very hard for your souls . . .' On and on he goes. He's giving us two weeks of detentions, early bed and no visits, and through the window we see Erik climbing into a taxi with his suitcase. A train will take him to the airport. He's going home, over the sea to Sweden. It's one of the worst days in my life. He believed in us, but he was wrong. We're hopeless. I'm thirteen and Psycho's right, I'll never amount to anything. Soon my gran will be dead and I'll still be here. Maybe I'll spend my whole life like this, and on my grave it'll say, CAR-DEVIL-DEKKO – LOSER.

Then comes surprise news and I ring Gran to tell her. 'Guess what, Gran, Mr Eriksonn's coming back! He only went to see his mum.' I never knew teachers had mums. I suppose they have to get here somehow.

He walks in and smiles. Gets us together and says sorry. 'It was my mistake. Stupid of me to take you there where you would feel intimidated and inferior. You're good boys. What do you say we try again?'

Good boys. There he goes again. Soft in the head.

'But, sir, Psycho'll never buy it.'

'Go and see him, nice and polite – tell him you will work hard and prove him wrong and make Hilljoy proud.'

'Get lost, sir, no way.'

We hold out for a week. 'You talk to him, sir, he'll listen to you.'

'He won't listen to me. He thinks I'm too soft.'

'Yes – well . . .'

Bed-time. I take out my picture of Mum and look at it. Steps at my back. A hand on my shoulder. 'It's OK to cry, boy.'

I can't cry. I won't cry.

We knock on Psycho's door. He can't believe his ears. 'Enter that tournament, after the last time? You must think I'm completely mad!'

'Now that you mention it, sir . . .'

'What was that, Declan?'

'I was going to say your prayers have worked, sir.'

'What do you mean?'

'We're reformed characters. We want to do it right this time. Jesus always gives sinners another chance.'

'What would you know about Jesus, Declan?'

'My gran loves Jesus, sir, so he can't be all that bad.'

Poor old Psycho, he's tearing his hair out. With Jesus looking over his shoulder he gives in. 'I can't believe I'm saying yes. I know you're going to let me down!'

We train hard. We practise controlling our tempers. ('Excuse me, pal, those are *my* shins you're kicking!')

and minding our manners ('Whoops, I'm so sorry, let me help you up!') We want to make it up to Erik. We want to prove to *ourselves* that we're not completely useless. But when the big day comes we're all scared, because deep down we feel useless, and we're bound to mess up again. The tournament's taking place at some sports centre: sixteen under-fourteen teams including – wait for it – Gretton!

In the first round we're drawn against some snotty little school called St Michael's. We're itching to smash their prim little faces, but we keep our tempers and our tongues and play quick, fast, direct football, and when the final whistle goes, we look at each other: 'Did we really win?'

Erik's furious. 'You must always shake hands when you win – you must be gentlemen.'

'We're gentlemen! gentle men! gentle gentlemen!' we sing.

We're in the last eight. Half-hour break and we're up against Marling High, known for miles around as Colditz. Look at them. They think they're well hard. They *are* well hard! Meaner-looking even than us – shaved heads, tattooed knuckles, ear-studs – *gangsters!* I feel small and lost.

'Relax, boys.' Erik draws us into a huddle. 'Remember, I don't care if you win or lose. Play beautiful football and hold your heads up.' He pats us, squeezes our shoulders.

'Get off!' says JB, who hates being touched.

'I'm sorry, I forgot,' says Erik. 'It's just I love you boys, and I want you to be happy.'

We swap glances. We feel calmer. Erik loves us. Did he really say *love*? We're not used to that word. Jesus loves us. We're told that every day. But for a person in this world to love us . . .

It's a brute of a game. They're hard and we're hard, and they're scared of us – you can see it in their eyes – and we're scared of them, so the football's terrible, and their teacher's going ape. You can see they're scared of him. When Mally equalizes their first goal, he goes ballistic. He doesn't love his boys like our Erik loves us. And – can you believe it? – with all the tackles thundering in, we keep our tempers and our tongues and they're the ones who crack. Mally's so tricky round the box, wiggling and weaving, they just *have* to bring him down – penalty! JB's such a cool penalty man: *smack* – 2–1!

It's a tight game. 2–1 at half time, and with Clubsy pulling off outrageous saves it stays 2–1. But we're tiring. They're fitter than us. Our lungs are sooty from all those ciggies. I'm gasping. All I can do to keep going is think of the maniac who knocked my mum down. They have a goal disallowed – they hit a post – Clubsy clears with a punch – the whistle saves us. We leap in the air. Erik shouts 'Boys!' and we remember our manners. I run to Colditz's captain. We shake hands.

On the outside I'm dead cool as always. Inside I'm shaking. I want to run into Mum's arms. I want to run to the dad I never had: 'We did it, we kept our shape, we beat a really good team.'

We're crazy happy, joking and laughing through lunch. Then we go quiet. We're playing Gretton – *Gretton!* – in the semis.

'We're knackered, sir,' I tell Erik.

'Pace yourselves for the first half. And remember, I don't care if you win or lose, so long as you play clean and beautiful.'

Gretton have had one hard game and one easy game. They look fresh and cool, like they've just stepped out of a Wash 'n' Go ad. They stand staring at us, trying to scare us. The ref brings together me and Gretton's captain Jack. As the coin spins, Jack the Ripper whispers: 'How many of you are taking an early shower this time?' and I tell him to get stuffed, and the ref warns me to watch my mouth.

We play clean and beautiful – crisp passes and balls into space like Erik taught us. And you've never seen such manners. I knock a man over, I give him a hand up. Jelly Beans fouls his man, he goes: 'Sorry, old bean, my mistake.' Then Smokes trips Jack up, gives him a hand up, and when the ref turns away, kicks Jack in the leg. To be fair to Smokes, he didn't start it. One of them – a tall ginger geezer with a sly grin and a mouth like Prince Charles – has been winding us up from the start: 'Where did you leave your ball and chain? Don't give the ball away, lads, they'll keep it!'

The goals go in like pinballs: 2–2 . . . 4–4 . . . 7–6

to them, and we're fading again, and they're starting to boss the game. My lungs are killing me. 'Give us another goal, God,' I pray, 'and I swear I'll never touch another ciggie.' The seconds are ticking down, the little crowd is shouting encouragement, and just as the ref's looking at his watch, Smokes fouls Ginger and hisses something so disgusting in his ear that Ginger sees red and throws a punch. The punch only glances Smokes, but Smokes goes down like a tree, and the ref sends Ginger off and they all crowd in arguing with the ref and one of them's swearing like a navvy and gets sent off. The little crowd claps and shouts. It's three of them against five of us. The ref looks at his watch again. There might just be time for—

The whistle's gone. We've lost. Tempers boil over and the teams have to be separated by Erik and Gretton's teacher and some priesty-bloke.

Erik drives us home. We're all wacked out. We've had a good time.

'You're in a mood, sir,' I say.

'I don't like the way you got those boys sent off.'

'They're wimps, they deserved it.'

'They're no different from you boys – no better, no worse. Deep down, we're all the same.'

It's two weeks since we lost to Gretton for the second time. Who cares? 7–6, 6–7, what difference does it make? Summer's come and the boys of Gretton and Colditz and St Michael's have gone home, and we're still here, hating the world and going nowhere. Erik's teaching us cricket, which is a laugh, 'cos he doesn't understand the rules.

I'm knocking on Psycho's door. 'Yes, Declan, what do you want?'

'I got to talk to you, sir.'

He looks up from his work: 'Pull up a pew.'

'I want to get out of here, sir.'

'Easier said than done, old chap.'

'I promise I won't attack any more cars.'

'Are you sure?'

'I want to start with yours, sir. It could do with a wash. It's Erik's idea.'

'Who's Erik, young man?'

'Mr Eriksonn, sir.'

Smithy, the caretaker, gives me a bucket and some cloths. I wash Psycho's car. The whole school stands and watches. 'Oi, Dekko,' Smokes whispers, 'want to borrow my screwdriver?' I ignore him. He'll be here for ever. But in three months or so I'll be saying goodbye to Erik and me mates and going home. Then the real test starts. When I see my mum's face over the fireplace at Gran's, will I run out in the street and take out my feelings on the first car I see. Or will I do like Erik says?

'*Don't be afraid to cry, boy.*'

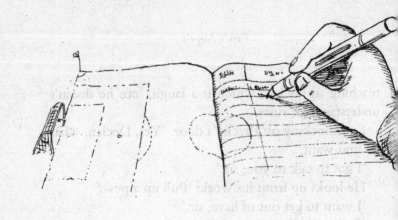

SOCCER DIARY
by Rob Childs

Monday 21 March

Hi there!

First day of spring – guess that's as good a day as any to start a diary. Better than most in fact 'cos this date's always extra special for me. It's my birthday! I'm now eleven years old.

Had loads of pressies. Best is a brand new England strip. Cool! At least it will be till they go and change their kit again.

This diary was a present from Gran. Says she's kept a diary ever since she was a little girl. Now she wants me to do the same. Only got another sixty years to go to catch her up! Might even get it published some day when I'm a rich, famous footballer. OK, so I'm dreaming. What's wrong with that? Don't suppose it'll ever happen, but you never know . . .

Soccer Diary

Used to think anybody who wrote stuff down in a diary all the time was well sad – never even knew Gran did it in secret – but this one's going to be different. It'll be my own soccer diary, a record of my career.

So let's kick off with our school's cup semi-final replay on Wednesday. Ashden Primary (that's us) v. Northfield Juniors, a tough lot from across town. Can't wait for that. Tell you more about it next time. Nearly run out of space on the page – and all this writing don't half make your hand ache. Been a good day – apart from having to go to school of course.

See ya!

'I just want a brief meeting to sort out a few things for the match tomorrow and then you can all go outside for break,' Mr Mackenzie told the Ashden soccer squad.

'Huh!' grunted Ali, the captain, under his breath. 'No chance.'

The footballers reckoned that their teacher's team meetings probably went on longer than the England manager's. He liked drawing tactical diagrams on the blackboard and began doing one now, putting little crosses for their own players and circles for their opponents.

'Set pieces,' he said. 'That's where I think Northfield are weak. They didn't mark us up very well last time.'

'Who's going to take the corners, Mr Mackenzie?' asked Dan, their most skilful midfield player. 'Me or Phil?'

'It depends whether Phil plays in goal or on the wing.

95

I'll put the team up on the board this lunch-time after I've given it a bit more thought.'

The players exchanged glances. They'd hoped to find out what the team was at this meeting. Nobody wanted to be left out of the big match with a place in the final at stake.

The teacher continued with his drawing. 'These arrows show some decoy runs you could make at corners to shake off any markers, and the dotted line is the path of the ball—'

'Which cross is supposed to be me?' Ali interrupted cheekily.

'This one at the far post,' said Mr Mackenzie, darting an irritated look at the boy over his spectacles. 'I'll put a number nine on it for you, shall I, Ali?'

The others chuckled, enjoying the usual sparring contest between the two. Ali was Ashden's leading scorer and boasted to his teammates that he knew more about the game than the teacher. Even Mr Mackenzie seemed to sense that too. When he was refereeing, he often left most of the half-time team talk to the captain.

'Yes, Phil?' asked the teacher, seeing the raised hand.

'Am I going to be in goal, Mr Mackenzie?'

'I'm not sure yet. You're our surprise package,' he said with a smile. 'They haven't seen you play yet. We might start off with you on the right wing first and see if your speed can catch them out.'

The captain grinned. 'Yeah, that way we can keep Sameer in goal,' he said. He preferred to ignore the fact that his best mate had been at fault for both of Northfield's equalizers in last week's 2–2 draw.

'Hmm, maybe,' Mr Mackenzie mused aloud. 'Then if we're ahead at half-time, we could switch Phil into goal to give us a better chance of holding onto the lead. How about that?'

'What if we're losing?' said Ali, being deliberately provocative.

'Then it means you've not been doing your job properly, captain,' he replied in retaliation. 'You'll have to start scoring some goals!'

Ali didn't think that was very funny. Nor was he amused as the meeting dragged on until the bell was heard in the playground for the end of morning break.

Tuesday 22 March

Hi there!

Back again! Nearly forgot to write this in all the excitement. Not used to having a diary yet. What a week! We're playing Northfield twice in four days – tomorrow's cup replay first and then in a crunch league game on Saturday. Last match of the season, that is – unless we make the final after Easter, of course – and we've got to win it to avoid relegation. We've not had the most successful season ever, as you can tell, apart from the cup run. That's why this replay's so important to us.

I missed the first semi-final game 'cos of a stupid cold. Almost screamed the house down when Mum said I wasn't fit to go to school that day. Felt like I was letting everybody down. Just a good job we didn't lose.

Mac's picked me to play right-wing, but I'll probably end up in goal. Mac — that's Mr Mackenzie, our sports teacher, by the way — can never decide where best to play me. Being big-headed for a minute — and you're allowed to brag a bit in your own diary — he reckons I'm the best keeper we've got, but I'm fast too and can shoot with both feet. That's the problem. I like scoring goals and I like stopping them, but I can't be in two places at the same time, can I?

Tell you what happens tomorrow night. Got to get my beauty sleep. I sure need it! Wish us luck.

See ya!

'Two–nil!' Ali groaned as the Ashden players gathered together at half-time. 'This is rubbish! We've hardly had a kick up front yet.'

'Speak for yourself,' Phil whined. 'That kid marking me keeps gouging great chunks out of my legs.'

'They don't dare try that with me,' Ali scoffed.

'Pity old Mac's not the ref today,' said Dan. 'He'd have soon put a stop to all their fouling.'

Mr Mackenzie joined their group at last, wanting to make a few points himself. 'Don't let their rough stuff upset you. Just keep trying to play your football. Let's see you knocking that ball about better.'

'And get it up to us in attack quicker,' Ali demanded of his teammates. 'We can't score if you don't give us the ball.'

'You might have to work harder to go and get it

yourself,' said Mr Mackenzie. 'It's no good just blaming other people.'

Ali went into a sulk, making it obvious he didn't approve of the tactical changes Mr Mackenzie was trying to put into effect. One was to replace Sameer in goal with Phil.

'If we can stop them scoring again,' the teacher reasoned, 'we might yet be able to get back into this game.'

The visitors' giggles when they saw who'd gone in goal were soon stifled. Twice the new keeper pulled off smart saves to prevent them increasing their lead, but they continued to pile on the pressure. Phil had never been so busy, bombarded from all angles with shots and crosses.

The home side could barely manage to clear the ball out of their own half and Ali became more and more frustrated. He stood alone in the centre circle, hands on hips, shouting complaints at his team. 'C'mon!' he cried. 'Sort it out. You're letting them walk all over you.'

Finally, the captain decided he'd have to go and show them how to do it himself. He charged into the penalty area like a snorting dragon, fires blazing, and clattered the opposing number nine as he was about to shoot.

'Penalty!' screamed all the Northfield players and the referee obediently pointed to the spot.

Ali glared around, challenging anyone to criticize him. Nobody dared. 'You'd better save this,' he muttered to Phil. 'Sameer would.'

The goalkeeper ignored his remark and settled on the line, waiting for the penalty-taker to move in and wondering which way to dive.

The referee blew his whistle for the duel to begin . . .

Wednesday 23 March
Hi there!

Faced my first penalty of the season today. Well, my first ever penalty actually in a proper match. Decided to dive to the right as this kid did a jinking kind of run up, trying to fool me. He did as well – the ball went to my left. I felt dead stupid.

Would have been nice to write that I'd saved a penalty and we won the match, but I guess that only happens in stories. We lost 3–1. Captain Ali scored our goal near the end, but you should have seen the dirty look he gave me when the penalty went in. I know he's not exactly my biggest fan, but it wasn't all my fault. I mean, he's the one who gave it away in the first place with a wild tackle.

So we're out the cup. No cup final for us to look forward to now. Shame! Instead of a medal, I've got bruises up both legs as souvenirs of my efforts on the wing before half-time. Think their full-back's hobby must be kicking people up in the air. Can't wait for Saturday now to get our revenge on Northfield.

Pity this diary's had to start off with a bad defeat, but guess that's football for you. 'You can't win 'em all,' old Mac said afterwards – and he's right for once. Bet I'll dream tonight that I was the big hero, saving that penalty. Hope so.

See ya!

★   ★   ★

The players were out on the pitch again on Friday for their usual lunch-time practice session. The previous day had been spent licking their wounds, but now they had to prepare for their survival battle in the league.

Ali certainly didn't want Ashden to end up being relegated, if only for the sake of his own pride. 'We've got to play much harder,' he demanded. 'Match them for the physical stuff.'

'Don't get dragged down to their level,' Mr Mackenzie insisted. 'I'm ref for the league match and they won't be allowed to get away with things. And nor will any of you lot. It's no good playing dirty. You saw what happened, Ali, when you tried to mix it with them.'

The captain scowled. 'I went for the ball. He just happened to get in the way, that's all.'

'Probably better in future if you stay out of our own penalty area,' the teacher said, unable to hide a mischievous grin. 'We need you causing havoc at the other end.'

The footballers worked on some set-piece moves, hoping they might actually be able to earn a few corners and free kicks this time. Phil and Dan took turns to hit the ball across, but only once did it really click. Ali timed his run to the far post to perfection and met Phil's curling centre with a powerful header past Sameer into the bottom corner.

'Excellent! We'll have another one of those tomorrow,' beamed Mr Mackenzie. 'I know it's the Easter holidays now, but early to bed tonight, please, everyone. Get plenty of sleep. You'll need all the energy you've got in the morning.'

Friday 25 March

Hi there!

Sorry about missing yesterday. Had to stay up late to finish a project for school and didn't feel like doing the diary after that – especially 'cos I was still down about losing in the cup. OK again now, though. It's end of term at last! Cool!!

Sorry about all these exclamation marks too. Bad habit of mine! Teacher says my spelling and sentences are good, but I've got to try and cut down on these things in stories!!!!! Pity! I like them! But I can do what I want in my own diary – Gran says so!

Back to the soccer. Mac's made a few team changes and I'm starting off in goal this time. It'll keep me away from that fouling full-back at least. Mac's even picked a girl in midfield. He likes having girls in the side when they're good enough and Laura's got a decent left foot. I get on with her OK, but Ali's not too keen. I could tell by his face when Mac announced the line-up this lunch-time after the practice. Tough! Ali won't mind if she goes and sets him up to score the winning goal.

Bet you know what I'm going to dream about tonight. Dead right!

See ya!

* * *

Northfield began the match as if they were chasing the league and cup double instead of being safely in mid-table. They launched a series of fierce attacks and it was only Phil's athletic goalkeeping that kept the scoreline blank.

'Great stop, Phil!' cried Laura as another goal-bound effort was safely pouched.

Phil grinned. 'Thanks. Go on, take it away up the left.'

The keeper rolled the ball into Laura's path and watched as she linked up well with Dan along the touchline before passing inside to the captain. Ali took it in his stride, beat a defender but then his shot was turned away for a corner, their first of the game.

'Remember what we planned,' hissed Mr Mackenzie as Dan trotted past him towards the corner flag to take the kick.

The referee was well-positioned to admire Ali's soaring leap to meet the ball, but had to swallow his disappointment as the captain's header grazed the crossbar.

It was Ashden's best chance of the first half. Northfield had dominated most of it and almost went ahead right on the stroke of half-time. A volley from inside the area took a late deflection off a defender, but Phil stuck out a leg in desperation and knocked the ball away.

Ali gave the goalie a little pat on the shoulder at the

interval. 'Saved us there,' he said. 'Keep it up.'

'Might be on the pitch second half.'

He shook his head. 'Nah. We need you more in goal. We've had it if they go and score.'

It was as near as the captain had come all season to acknowledging that Phil was a better keeper than Sameer.

'A draw's no good to us,' Mr Mackenzie reminded his team. 'We've got to win to stay up. If the score's still level after a while, we'll have to take risks.'

After a quarter of an hour of the second period the situation was unchanged. The referee blew his whistle to halt play and make a substitution. 'Right, Phil, get that top off,' he called out. 'Play right-wing, please.'

Phil had come prepared. The visitors watched the swap with interest, but in an instant the yellow goalie top was peeled off to reveal Ashden's light-blue shirt underneath.

Sameer took Phil's place between the posts somewhat nervously, but soon felt a good deal more relaxed after he clung onto a firmly hit drive that tested out his reflexes.

The Northfield full-back leered at the new winger. 'Didn't think you'd fancy meeting me again.'

'You're right,' Phil grinned back. 'I don't fancy you at all!'

Suddenly, the match caught fire. Phil was clumsily brought down after trying to cut inside the full-back and the free kick made Mr Mackenzie's gamble pay off.

Phil swung the kick into the goalmouth and Ali threw himself in front of his marker to make first contact with the ball. His glancing header was steered into the net between the keeper and a defender on the goal line.

His wild celebrations knew no bounds and it was a struggle for Mr Mackenzie to get the captain and the rest of the team to focus their minds back onto the game. 'C'mon, concentrate,' he urged them. 'The match isn't over till I blow the final whistle. We haven't won it yet.'

Stung into retaliation, Northfield swarmed all over Ashden in search of the equalizer. After Sameer fumbled one shot and another smacked against the woodwork, Mr Mackenzie decided that Phil had to go back in goal. Sameer found himself moved out to play in defence instead.

Sadly, no sooner had Phil pulled the yellow jersey back on than the visitors finally broke their duck. Neither Phil, nor Sameer – nor even both of them together – could have prevented the goal. It was a viciously swirling strike that whooshed into the top corner of the net well out of reach.

Mr Mackenzie groaned and looked at his watch. There were only three minutes left. He contemplated switching Phil yet again but felt that enough was enough. Their chance had gone.

Northfield swept forward once more, tearing open the home defence with a swift-passing move that left an attacker with only the goalkeeper to beat. Phil raced out to meet him and timed the dive at his feet superbly. The ball rolled loose from the collision out of the penalty area.

'Don't pick it up!' screamed Sameer. 'Kick it clear.'

Phil seemed in a bit of a daze at first, uncertain perhaps what to do as two opponents closed in. Nobody could quite believe what happened next. The goalkeeper tricked both players with a neat piece of footwork and then set off with the ball upfield, gathering speed.

'Have you gone crazy?' yelled Ali. 'Get back in goal!'

Saturday 26 March

Hi there!

Had to come to bed early, I'm so tired. Writing this propped up on my pillows. What an incredible game! Still can't get over what I went and did right near the end.

The score was 1–1 when I bombed out of goal to stop them scoring their second and found myself with the ball at my feet. Guess instinct just took over. It must have looked pretty weird to see the goalie go flying up the wing! Their full-back tried to foul me again but he was too slow. Sold him a lovely dummy and left him on his fat backside before I suddenly burnt out. My legs just turned to jelly. I managed to pass the ball inside to Laura and then collapsed in a heap.

Didn't even see the goal. They told me later that Laura's shot was blocked and Dan scored the winner from the rebound. So we did it – we're safe!

The celebrations afterwards were great – apart from one

thing. I hate my full name. I've banned everybody from using it, even the teachers, but Ali sometimes comes out with it to tease me. Could have killed him when he started up this chant in the cloakroom.

'One Phil-o-me-na! There's only one Phil-o-me-na!'

He's right, though. I'm the only girl in the school called Philomena. Possibly the only one in the town – or even the whole county – with that name for all I know!

Ah, never mind, sweet dreams at last. Reckon I've deserved them, don't you?

See ya!

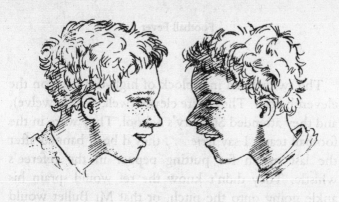

TURN THE OTHER CHEEK

by Aivlys L. Hardy

There was nothing other than ordinary about Dillon and Mat Murphy. Except, maybe, that they were twins. Identical twins with bright red hair and blue eyes. Of course, they liked football . . . no, actually, they didn't just like it, they *lived* for it. The only thing that came anywhere close to football in their lives was playing practical jokes.

Dillon and Mat liked a bit of fun, but their jokes had a way of backfiring on them. Take the maggots, for instance. The twins had found the tin of maggots on the canal bank. Having rescued them, they took the maggots to school to rehouse them in the headteacher's desk drawer. Mr Bullet did *not* find it funny to see maggots squirming in his drawer, lurking between papers and squelching in his sandwiches!

109

The twins lived in a block of high-rise flats, on the eleventh floor. They were eleven (well, nearly twelve), and they attended St Mary's School. They were in the football team. I say *were* . . . they'd been banned after the last match for putting pepper in the referee's whistle. They didn't know the ref would sprain his ankle going onto the pitch, or that Mr Bullet would take over as referee *and* borrow the whistle. Bullet was not amused. They'd have got away with it if Joseph Jackson hadn't snitched on them. Snitcher JJ told their deadly enemies, Jake and Franklyn. They told Bullet.

Bullet went ballistic. '*Murphy twins!* You're *out* of the school team.'

At first, the team was furious with JJ, Jake and Franklyn, because Dillon and Mat were the best scorers in the team. 'Why did you tell Bullet?' Stinky Watts yelled.

'He said there'd be no football till he found out who'd put pepper in the whistle,' Jake yelled back.

'Oh yeah! You just wanted our place in the team,' Dillon snapped.

'At least we play football, not stupid jokes!' Franklyn smirked.

'Franklyn's right! Anyway, your jokes always cause trouble— *Aah!*' JJ squealed as Mat kicked his shin.

'It's true!' Jake snarled. 'We all got detention because *you* put maggots in Bullet's desk . . . no-one snitched then.'

'But the twins are our best scorers,' Stinky said, as if it excused everything.

'*Were* the best scorers,' Franklyn gloated. 'Me and Jake are now!'

The team grumbled. Stinky growled, '*You'll* never be as good as the twins . . . You'd better not let the team down.'

'*They* let us down. Bullet says so,' Jake retorted.

'Bullet's right,' JJ ventured, rubbing his shin and watching Mat. The rest of the team muttered: for once they had to agree with JJ. So now the team was furious with the twins for playing jokes and getting slung off the team. Dillon and Mat had nowhere to go and nothing to do.

'No more football – ever,' Mat groaned.

'It's the end of the world,' Dillon said.

Until . . .

'I'm at my wits' end. I don't know what to do with them. I begged Mr Bullet to let them back in the team but he said no: "Definitely no. It's the last straw, they've been warned often enough." Lord knows what those two'll do next. I fear for them, Father Paul. I really do.' Mrs Murphy took a deep breath.

'Calm yourself, dear Mrs Murphy. Boys will be boys, you know.'

'*I* know that better than most, Father Paul.'

'Yes. Of course you do. Your boys aren't bad, they're . . . boisterous. They need an outlet.'

111

'I'll give them outlet!' Mr Murphy grunted from behind the *Daily Scorch*.

'As I was saying, Mrs Murphy . . . They're boisterous, they need something to keep them busy. How about the church choir?' One look at Mrs Murphy made Father Paul swallow hard and try again. 'Perhaps not. Well, I do need a couple of players for the church youth football team. We're playing St Pancras on Saturday. We need all the help we can get against *them*. They're top of the league.'

'Just the ticket,' Mrs Murphy said.

So it was settled. Mat and Dillon were to play for St Petroch's Church youth team. Training at five o'clock sharp on the recreation ground.

'And don't let me down. This is your last chance. You cause any problems for Father Paul and you're banned from football *for life*!' she threatened as the twins left the flat at four-thirty.

'Poxy Petroch's,' Dillon grumbled.

'It's almost worse than *no* football,' Mat sulked.

'We're jinxed, Mat. Jinxed.'

'Or cursed. D'you suppose Father Paul put the hex on us so's we have to play for his rotten team? They haven't won a game all season and now they're up against St Pancras, last year's league champions.'

'It'll be lambs to the slaughter. Anyone fouling and Father Paul'll be saying, "Turn the other cheek, boys. Turn the other cheek."'

'Yeah! While St Pancras knocks the stuffing out of us.'

'Wait till Jake and Franklyn hear about it. They'll never stop laughing at us. I can hear them now, "Poxy, pimply Petroch's".'

Father Paul shook hands with the twins. 'Welcome to St Petroch's youth team. I think you all know each other. Cedric's our captain. He'll make sure you're at home here. Come on, boys, let's get started.'

But church football wasn't quite like school football – or not the way the twins played it. Dillon deliberately tripped Cedric in a tackle – but there was no retaliation. Mat pushed Angelino, ruining his shot at goal – no resistance. Except that Father Paul blew the whistle for the twentieth time in the match. This time he beckoned Mat and Dillon to his side. In quiet, confidential tones he said, 'Now, twins, I can't keep warning you. We don't do that kind of thing at St Petroch's . . . We don't want to let your mother down, do we?' He stared hard at each twin in turn and gave them a knowing wink.

'No, Father Paul,' they chorused limply.

'OK! Let's get some *real* football played here.'

Mat and Dillon exchanged glances. The game resumed. Mat ducked and weaved as Tich Tomkiss came in to tackle, then flicked the ball past and ran on – leaping over Tich. Mat raced down the wing and got a cross to Dillon, who slipped past Nick and put the ball past Brownie, in goal.

'Well done! That's the way to do it,' Father Paul

113

enthused, blowing the whistle for end of training. 'Terrific goal, twins. Hope you score like that against St Pancras! Jolly good. See you tomorrow, same time.'

It was no good telling Mum they'd pulled a hamstring, or strained a ligament, or fractured a collar bone. There was no way out of playing for St Petroch's and no way to avoid facing Jake and Franklyn the following morning . . .

'*School – now!*' Mum shrieked. 'Get on, the pair of you. Out from under my feet.'

Mat slammed the door and they slunk off down the concrete stairs and across the kiddies' playground. Mum would watch them all the way to the school gate from the balcony at Number 11. They felt her look burning their backs as they slouched into the school yard. Saved by the bell, they went straight into class. No-one said a word. There was an eerie silence right up until lunchtime. Then JJ sidled up to them saying, 'They've sent you to Coventry for playing stupid jokes.'

Dillon grabbed JJ by the throat. 'What?'

'Let go – you're choking me.'

'You're not blue yet!' Mat sniggered.

'What d'you mean?' Dillon snarled at him.

'That pepper in the ref's whistle. You two are the best scorers, but because of that joke you won't be playing in the tournament. So we won't win.'

Dillon shook him. 'What tournament?'

'The special one-day tournament for soccer sponsorship.'

'What are you on about, JJ?' Mat said, twisting his arm.

'Don't you know anything? The superstore tournament. The superstore's sponsoring the winning team for a year – new strip, pitch, minibus, the lot!'

Dillon and Mat dropped JJ, who made his escape as they stood, stunned by the revelation.

'And we're lumbered with poxy Petroch's!'

'Just our luck!' Mat kicked the cupboard door. *Crash!*

'You'll pay for that, Murphy!' Bullet roared, as the front shattered into fragments. 'Off the premises before you demolish anything else!'

They dived through the open door and ran. They didn't stop running until they reached the superstore car park. There on a noticeboard, for all the world to see, were the five-a-side team fixtures for church youth and school teams (drawn out of a hat, it said, by the Mayor) for the SPECIAL SUPERSTORE ONE-DAY SOCCER EXTRAVAGANZA. Dillon checked the list. 'St Petroch's is playing St Michael's in the first leg.'

'Why didn't Father Paul say?'

'I suppose it could've been worse. We might have been playing Bog End Road.' Dillon grimaced. 'Or St Mary's!'

The Saturday match didn't make them feel any better. The game against St Pancras ended in a score of 5–0. And it wasn't St Petroch's who scored five. St Pancras stormed the pitch like escaped tigers.

Cedric ended up with a broken arm, Angelino got a black eye, St Pancras got three goals from penalties given against Dillon, and Mat got sent off for kicking the goalie. But despite their best efforts, neither of the twins sustained any physical injuries!

'Well, boys,' Father Paul said after the slaughter. 'You did your best. We can't ask for better than that. It's the playing that counts, not the winning.'

'It's the winning that counts for the superstore tournament,' Dillon blurted out.

'Well, we've three days of half-term before the game. We'll train every day.'

Mat groaned. The prospect of three days' intensive training with this lot was the pits.

'Every day, boys. With a good heart. If we want something badly enough, we'll work for it and get it. We want a proper pitch and Lord knows, we could do with a new strip.'

'And boots,' Tich Tomkiss piped up, looking at the gaping toe in his.

'Boots as well,' Father Paul said. 'But there's some good news, boys. While the work at the rec goes ahead over half-term next week and the pitch is unusable, Mr Bullet says we can use St Mary's School pitch for training.'

The team cheered. The twins groaned.

St Petroch's youth team turned up at the school on the first morning of half-term. Jake and Franklyn were there, hanging around, sniggering at the twins. Bullet

116

arrived in his red BMW. 'I'm watching you, Murphy twins!' he warned as they kicked off.

Father Paul put St Petroch's through their paces. By the end of the session the team were shattered. The twins' heads were spinning from game plans and tactics – limbs aching from weaving, turning, sprinting. They staggered home for lunch, too tired to even notice Snitcher JJ sneaking around the back of the school buildings . . .

Mum slopped baked beans on their toast. '*Eat!* Father Paul wants to see you again at three o'clock. At the rec, this time. It had better not be trouble! If you've caused problems for Father Paul you're *banned from football for life!*'

The food stuck in their throats.

But worse was to follow as Father Paul arrived at the rec that afternoon, a grim look on his face.

'Bad news, boys.' He looked at the boys in a way that made them know he was *very* serious. 'Mr Bullet has had a tyre slashed on his car this morning. He accuses Dillon and Mat.'

The twins gaped in amazement, Mum's words ringing in their ears – 'Any problems for Father Paul and you're banned from football for life!'

Father Paul raised an eyebrow and kept talking. 'He has witnesses.'

'He can't have . . . we didn't do it!' Dillon exploded.

Father Paul paused but had more to say before he would listen to the twins.

Mat hissed to Dillon, 'Jake and Franklyn!'

'Even they wouldn't do something *that* bad to stop us playing football – would they?' Dillon whispered.

Father Paul seemed to ignore them. '*If* you apologize to Mr Bullet, he'll let us use the pitch. No apology means no training.' He glanced over at a digger on the rec. 'That means no tournament for St Petroch's!'

The St Petroch's team glared at the twins; everything hinged on their apology . . . but for once they weren't to blame. Father Paul waited.

Dillon cleared his throat. 'Honest, Father Paul . . .' he began. He glanced at Mat. Together they continued, 'Honest. We didn't slash the tyre.'

'The twins were with us. They couldn't have done it . . . not unless they went back after training,' Cedric said, nursing his plastered arm.

'They could just apologize anyway . . .' Tich chimed in.

'Not if they didn't do it,' Nick said. 'It'd be better not to be in the tournament than make them own up to something they haven't done. Why should anyone be bullied into apologizing for something they didn't do?'

'I agree with Nick,' Angelino remarked. 'But then we'll need a miracle if we want to be in the tournament.'

Everyone watched the twins, waiting.

Dillon couldn't believe the team weren't angry and blaming them. He cleared his throat. 'If we've got to apologize . . .' He looked at Mat for support.

Mat was thinking hard and deciding that the best way to show Bullet and St Mary's was to win – win with St Petroch's. Mat nodded to Dillon; he knew they were both thinking the same thing.

Dillon spoke for both of them. 'If we've got to apologize – for the sake of the team – we will.'

Father Paul scrutinized each twin carefully. Everyone felt uncomfortable with the 'no win' situation they were all in. Then he said, 'That's settled then. Angelino, we need that miracle. We won't be using St Mary's pitch for training.'

The team looked puzzled.

'Nick's right. Turning the other cheek is one thing, but owning up to something you didn't do is quite another. I believe the twins! They're practical jokers – not vandals. That's an end to it. Now, let's pray for a miracle.' Father Paul looked heavenward . . .

'Problems, Father Paul?' Sister Sophie squeaked at his elbow.

'You could say that, sister.' Father Paul waved his arm, like Moses at the Red Sea, towards the gaping hole sliced across the rec.

'Oh, my!' Sister Sophie smiled as she looked at the dispirited bunch of would-be footballers. 'You're not having much luck at St Petroch's.'

'You can say that again,' Dillon blurted.

'Sister Sophie stared hard at him. 'Dillon Murphy, I think. Do you happen to know anything about Sister

119

Amelia's rosary? She was at the hospital two hours while they got her fingers unstuck from the beads . . . you didn't see how the glue got there, did you?'

For the first time in his life, Dillon blushed. So did Mat. Muffled snorts sounded amongst the team. So did a muffled 'Sorry'.

Sister Sophie smiled. 'Well, no real harm done, I suppose. Sister Amelia – she's keen on football: we have a team at St Xavier's, thanks to her. A pretty good pitch too – it was our croquet lawn. You could use the convent pitch, Father Paul – perhaps we could even play a friendly game tomorrow. What do you say?'

The friendly against the nuns provided *plenty* of training in turning the other cheek. The sisters – though they played a good game and had an ace scorer in Sister Sophie – got away with some sly tricks! Shirt-tugging, tripping – you name it, they did it. Each time the boys went to retaliate Father Paul would shout, 'Turn the other cheek, boys. Shake hands now and play on.'

As if that wasn't bad enough, Sister Amelia was the referee. Every time Dillon tackled Sister Frances the whistle went for a free kick or a penalty. He shook hands *frequently*. Mat got sent off for tripping Sister Agatha – he caught his boot in her habit when she came flying out of goal, just as he kicked the ball. She winked as they shook hands.

'Good game, boys,' the nuns laughed as the whistle went for full-time. 'Six–one. It was a nice goal you scored, Nick. Not many get past Sister Agatha!' And they filed off to Evensong.

Dillon grinned. 'That's all we need.'

'Poxy Petroch's and the Soul Sisters,' Mat laughed, kicking a lump of clay. *Thud!* 'St Xavier!' the nuns chorused from inside the chapel, as the stained-glass window shuddered. Dillon and Mat fled down the convent drive.

The day of the tournament dawned. The Seven Pitches sports ground was full. The twins jostled their way to the changing rooms. St Mary's team jeered and whistled as they walked past. Bullet glowered.

'There you are, twins. Come on, get your kit on,' Father Paul greeted them. They stared in amazement: there were new boots on the locker and, hanging on the pegs, gold shirts emblazoned with deep purple crosses. 'From the sisters – for being good sports about the friendly.'

'Wow!' exclaimed Dillon. 'We look like a real team now.'

Father Paul smiled. 'By the way, a St Mary's boy – Joseph Jackson – had a chat with Sister Amelia. It seems he saw Jake and Franklyn vandalize Mr Bullet's car. Apparently Mr Bullet wouldn't listen to him. OK! St Petroch's, do your best. And, remember . . .'

'Turn the other cheek,' the team chanted.

Whether it was the sisters' gift, prayers or the extra training, St Petroch's weren't sure, but they got through to the semi-final. Even in their first game against St Michael's the tips Brownie had learned from Sister Agatha seemed to work – only one shot got past him. Tich fired a low ball into the corner of the net, scoring one of the two St Petroch's goals, Mat heading in the other from Nick's teasing cross – the like of which they'd only seen from Sister Frances.

In the semi-final they faced their old rivals – St Pancras. St Petroch's were soon reminded of their 5–0 defeat as St Pancras tamed the ball, attacking at a furious pace and upsetting St Petroch's defence. By half-time they were shattered – a goal down and demoralized.

Father Paul was the only one smiling. 'Cheer up, St Petroch's. Even the sisters would find St Pancras a hard team to beat!' Then he laughed. 'Who needs to win anyway?'

'We do!' Tich said. 'We *need* our own pitch.'

St Petroch's didn't need any further encouragement, but St Pancras were equally determined to win. They roared into action with a quick chance at goal – Mallory sent Brownie flying the wrong way but somehow he managed to just flick out his left foot and push the ball wide of the post. It gave St Petroch's the spur they needed to take charge of the game. Dillon went on the attack: he cleared a high ball to Nick, who slammed in a header, sending the St Pancras goalie scrambling to punch the ball away. Mat got a touch to it, putting it safely into the corner of the net. *Goal!*

With St Pancras in disarray following this un-expected equalizer, Mat stormed down the pitch in search of a second goal. And it wasn't long in coming: a neat one-two with Dillon, a flick on to Nick and *bang*. St Petroch's were in the lead. When the final whistle went, St Petroch's were through to the final by a whisker, two goals to one.

However, in the other semi-final – St Mary's v. Bog End Road – both sides looked unbeatable.

'Which'd be worse?' Dillon said.

'Dunno.' Mat straightened his gold shirt. 'What d'you reckon to St Petroch's?'

'They've got the best scorers!'

The twins laughed and Mat said, 'Yeah! Let's win this tournament!'

They watched their opposition battling it out.

'The linesman must be blind – Jake kicked that kid!'

'Franklyn's just punched the goalie . . . where's the ref?'

The ref was being stretchered off, having got in the way of a crafty head butt from Stinky Watts.

A new referee came on. 'Sister Amelia!' Dillon and Mat gasped.

Bog End scored so fast that JJ didn't see it coming, but St Mary's equalized minutes later. Chants rang round the pitch as the game swung to and fro, with Bog End scoring, then St Mary's, until it was three all.

Bullet was furious: he couldn't bear the thought of

his team losing. He paced the sideline. 'Come on, St Mary's, get stuck in!'

Jake fouled a defender. The whistle blew. 'Free kick to Bog End.'

Sister Amelia was speaking to Bullet on the sideline, asking him to calm down.

Play went on and Bog End scored again. The whistle sounded for half-time.

Sister Amelia went over to the St Mary's team, appealing to them to keep the game clean. Bullet was in a frenzy: he wanted his team to win and he didn't care how. He turned his back on Sister Amelia and let rip at them.

Five minutes into the second half and Bog End were still 4–3 ahead. Jake passed to Franklyn, but Franklyn lost out to Bog End, who powered forward. Buster Bates went in with a flying tackle and the whistle went, but Stinky Watts continued to dribble down the field, sending a cross to Jake. Bullet was yelling, 'Go on, Jake. Get stuck in.' Jake dashed on, elbowing the Bog End defender aside, and again the whistle went for the foul. Jake pounded on. The whistle blew again, and Sister Amelia ran across to make Jake stop. He barged into her, deliberately pushing her over.

The crowd held their breath. Bullet rushed onto the pitch. 'Out of the way, ref.' He snatched the whistle from her. 'Stick to what you're good at, sister! Play on. Obstruction! St Mary's free kick.' The crowd began jeering, shouting, whistling. The players were motionless as Bullet yelled, 'Play on. Play on!'

Sister Amelia picked herself up, strode over to Bullet, tapped him on the shoulder, took the whistle off him and, in a voice like thunder, said, 'Off! You and your team of thugs. Off! You're out of the tournament.'

So that's how St Mary's were knocked out – and how Saint Petroch's came to play Bog End Road in the final of the tournament. The teams were pretty evenly matched, though Bog End were a bit free with the sort of play that St Petroch's didn't go in for.

St Petroch's began well: their offensive strategy went like a dream, but Bog End were cunning masters of dirty tactics. In the first five minutes, Dillon made one good break, but was blocked by a tackle from the Bog End skipper, who put in a jab for good measure to slow him down. Mat took the free kick, sending a high ball to Nick, who nodded it on to Tich in midfield. Dillon was shouting for the ball now and some neat short passes between him and Tich confounded Bog End, leaving their defence standing as Tich finally hammered the ball into the goal.

One–nil to St Petroch's. But Bog End equalized soon after with a corner, and the action thundered up and down the pitch until the half-time whistle blew at 1–1.

The sisters appeared on the sideline for the second half. 'Come on, St Petroch's.' Sister Sophie's squeak came over loud and clear as Tich took the first corner of the half. Sister Agatha stood behind the goal at the other end, giving instructions to Brownie as Bog End won the ball and raced down, their number nine in with a good chance of scoring. Chasing back in support of the defence, Dillon put in a good strong tackle, winning back the ball and then clearing it past the halfway line.

And so it went on, both teams evenly matched, and both determined to win. But neither side could get that vital goal that would clinch the tournament.

Until, only minutes from the final whistle . . . Angelino had come on as substitute and he and Tich were running well, passing like clockwork. The goal was in sight, the Bog End defence momentarily confused. The nuns roared the team on. Mat and Dillon moved forward, Tich passed to Mat, back to Dillon, Angelino rose for the header. Mat was in position, shouting, but as Angelino jumped for the ball, a Bog End defender matched his leap, heads cracked and the Bog End player poked Angelino in the eye as the two players crumpled towards the ground. A groan went up from the crowd. Sister Frances covered her eyes in despair.

St Petroch's felt very frustrated. They'd suffered bruised shins, shirt-tugging – the Bog End team were every bit as skilled in dirty tactics as the nuns at St Xavier's. Seeing the tournament now slipping away from them, St Petroch's were ready to do *anything* to win.

The Bog End boys saw the collision as a foul against them and were furious at the ref's decision – free kick to St Petroch's. Their players turned to mark the St Petroch's players, taunting and goading them, spoiling for a fight. Dillon realized that, if a fight broke out now, the game'd be over. He could feel it sliding away, like a second's worth of sand, slithering through an egg timer. He glanced at Mat: they had to try. Together they yelled, '*Turn the other cheek!*'

The St Petroch's players responded immediately. They shook hands with their aggressors, slapping their opponents on the shoulders and laughing. Bog End were simply flabbergasted. Mat moved onto the ball and took the free kick quickly, sliding it across to Dillon, who steadied it and snatched a look at goal. Bog End had woken from their trance and were moving into position. Mat sprinted towards Dillon yelling, 'Go for it! Shoot!' Dillon went for it. A long, curving, powerful blast of a shot. *Goal!*

The final whistle blew. The ground exploded, the crowd cheering, nuns leaping. St Petroch's team went crazy. Father Paul clasped his hands together and laughed until he cried. The twins were hoisted onto shoulders, carried round the pitch by *their* team – St Petroch's.

The superstore tournament cup was engraved: 'ST PETROCH'S CHURCH YOUTH FOOTBALL TEAM. *Turn the other cheek.*'

JANEY

by Dennis Hamley

Janey knew more about football than any of the boys in the school. She could quote every League and Premiership champion since 1947 and every Cup-winner since 1930. She knew every statistic about the World Cup and the European Championship since they were started. She could tell you the scorers in the 1972 European Cup Final and every other one as well. Boys would bring in year books and histories of the game and shoot questions at her: 'In the 1952 World Cup, where did England play the USA and what was the score?' Quick as a flash – 'In Brazil, Belo Horizonte, and the USA beat us one–nil.' 'Who were the first team after the war ended in 1945 to win the League two years running?' 'Portsmouth, of course.' Yes, ancient questions like that she got right without a

129

flicker of her eyelids. Most boys couldn't remember who won the FA Cup two years ago.

And it wasn't only history she knew about. Her brother Dale said it drove him and Dad mad watching football on TV with her. They'd be screaming for offside and she'd say calmly, 'He couldn't have been. The number six put him on-side.' The replay always showed she was right. They'd howl for a red card and she'd murmur, 'No, the defender went for the ball. The forward's making a meal of it.' Again the replay always showed that's what had happened, even if they could hear the writhing player screaming in agony two seconds before he loped away quite all right. 'She ruins it,' said Dale.

'Then tell her to bog off,' said Clive.

'How can we?' Dale answered.

How could they indeed?

Janey had a favourite team of her own. Sometimes, when the family stayed with an uncle and aunt who lived there, she watched them. She always came back ecstatic. So what was this team? Man United? Newcastle? Spurs?

'I went to see Doncaster Belles last week,' she'd say when she got back to school. 'Best women's football team in Britain.'

They knew better than to mock. Janey gave as good as she got.

'Who did they play then?' asked Clive the first time, laughing his head off. 'Liverpool Brownies?'

'Arsenal,' she said. 'The Belles won three–nil.' Before Clive could answer, she went on, 'And they could probably beat the men as well.'

'I don't doubt that,' said Darren.

Clive, who supported Arsenal passionately, forgot Janey and punched him.

Janey just smiled to herself and got on with what she was doing. She wasn't daft, either.

Janey might drive Dale and Dad round the twist sometimes and enrage Clive as well, but everybody thought the world of her. She was small and thin, with large brown eyes. If she'd played football herself she would want the ball to her feet, to dance past defenders and get out of the way of the most savage of tackles. She would have known how to keep out of trouble. She would have been a great passer of the ball, spot-on from thirty yards. You could tell that somehow, just by looking at her and the way she moved.

So why did it look as though she could never play for the Doncaster Belles herself? Girls played football more and more; girls were allowed to play in the same teams as boys now. Mr Gaynor, in charge of football at Firth Park School, always said that if he found girls who were good enough he'd get rid of the boys without a second thought.

But if he ever did, Janey would probably not be among them.

Janey was ill. She had been for years. There was

something terribly wrong with her liver. For long periods she was away. 'She's in Great Ormond Street again,' Dale would say quietly.

And when she came back, she was pale, weak and subdued. Slowly she would seem to get better; colour would come back to her face. And then she would be away again, the 'get well' cards would be sent and they would try not to think of what she might be going through in that hospital far away.

That year, Firth Park School's football team was having a wonderful time. They played in the local school league and, from the start of the season, they had a feeling it was to be their year. School after school came to Firth Park to be rolled over; Firth Park set off to their pitches and always came back three or four goals to the good. Clive and Dale, Delroy and Sam, Darren and Sunil, Colin and Winston, Trevor, Steve and Lee, game after game in their bright red shirts – invincible. Always Janey was there. As the weather grew colder, she almost disappeared underneath woolly hat, red scarf, thick blue coat and black leggings. But she never missed – watching, not shouting, saving it all up.

When half-time came and Mr Gaynor gave his talk, Janey was there as well. 'That goalkeeper doesn't know whether to stay on his line or come out,' she would say. Or – 'That one out on the right, with the ginger hair. You're letting him get good crosses in. If you keep pushing him wide so he can't use his right foot, you'll cut him out of the game.' Or – 'That big defender with the crew-cut. He panics if someone runs at him. You could have their penalty area to yourselves if you make him nervous.'

And they took notice. In the second half they did what she said. It always worked. Two goals at least, directly from what Janey spotted.

'You're our mascot,' said Clive.

'What are you talking about?' said Winston. 'She's our manager.'

'If Gaynor's our coach,' said Darren, 'Janey's our director of football.'

Janey just smiled. She was dreaming of striding the pitch as the far-seeing playmaker for the Doncaster Belles. But unless she had an all-or-nothing hospital operation pretty soon, she would never even have a chance.

The season drew to a close. Two games to go; two points needed for Firth Park to win the league. Two draws would do it, but why not finish in style with a couple of big wins and show everybody who was boss? Besides, the last game was against St Boniface's, the only team who could catch them. It would be too nerve-racking if everything depended on the last game. It's better to challenge than be challenged.

What was the next match? Away to Prickly Gorse, from deep in the country. 'A right load of turnip-bashers,' said Clive. 'We'll eat them for breakfast.'

'And then St Boniface's can do what they like,' said Darren. 'They can't catch us.'

Perhaps they were talking too soon. Perhaps there was a little seed of doubt. Perhaps they needed to convince themselves.

For this would be the first match Janey had missed this season. Three days before, she had gone back into Great Ormond Street. All-or-nothing time for Janey was here and Dale was very quiet.

The minibus with Mr Gaynor driving wound through narrow country lanes. Prickly Gorse seemed miles from anywhere. The boys saw the few houses, the church, the little shop with CLOSED plastered all over the empty windows, then the old school buildings, the bumpy pitch and its rickety goal posts. 'We'll bury this lot, man,' yelled Delroy as the minibus turned into the playground. Then, almost automatically, he looked to where Janey usually sat next to Dale. 'Won't we?' he added, a hesitant question with no answer.

It was a blustery March day. They felt uncomfortable as they walked onto the rutted pitch. A row of Prickly Gorse kids and parents stood along the touchline next to the school. Seven mournful black and white cows stared at them over the fence on the other side.

'Is that the Toon Army?' said Trevor. Nobody found that funny.

They kicked off. Things went wrong at once. Dale in midfield won the ball. He came forward with it and looked up. To his right was Sam, to his left was Sunil. Both looked unmarked. He chose Sam to pass to. The pass was accurate enough but, as if from nowhere, a huge red-faced boy lumbered in the way of the ball and hoofed it first time towards the Firth Park goal. Clive tried to head it away, missed and saw it fall to a thin, gangling Prickly Gorse forward. He made as if to shoot towards the right of Trevor in goal. Trevor moved that way to cover the shot. But the ball spun off the outside of the forward's foot and bounced unevenly along the ground towards the left-hand corner. Trevor turned frantically and dived back across the goal. The ball hit a bobble, then his shoulder and rolled beyond his reach into the net.

'What were you doing, Dale?' shouted Sunil. 'I bet Janey would have told you to pass to me.'

Dale hung his head. He knew Sunil was right.

The spectators did not so much cheer as gasp with amazement. The cows chewed on unperturbed.

One down. Firth Park went all out for the equalizer. They couldn't go down to a fluke, surely? Darren met Delroy's cross from the right. He couldn't control the ball and that same beefy giant who had started the goal move burst across and thumped the ball into touch.

'You should have left it,' yelled Lee in frustration. 'I was clear on goal.' And then the dreaded addition: 'Janey would have told you to.'

Half-time. Glumly, the Firth Park team gathered round Mr Gaynor. He said his few words. They hardly listened: they could see that he had given them up for lost on that windy afternoon miles from home. Almost automatically, they looked round for Janey to tell them where they were going wrong, what to do about it, how to smash the scourge of the giant defender, the beanpole striker and all those other awkward characters who were making their lives misery.

But she wasn't there. They stared at empty air, as if Janey would materialize before them in a sudden column of whirling dust.

Fat chance. The whistle blew. They shambled back into position as if their fates were sealed. They were faltering at the last hurdle, they were blundering into defeat and they'd be so demoralized that St Boniface's would beat them next week and they'd lose the league at the last gasp.

Dale attempted a desperate piece of advice. 'Try to think what Janey would say,' he shouted as they lined up waiting for the whistle.

'And I'll take advice from my old granny,' yelled a Prickly Gorse player and his team fell about laughing so the ref had to delay the start of the second half.

When it did get under way, things were even worse. Prickly Gorse steamrollered through. The Firth Park players seemed to have forgotten what it was they were supposed to do. If Trevor tried to catch the ball, it fell limply out of his hands. If Dale went to clear first time, his boot swung at empty air and the ball bounced past. If Winston tried to head it, the ball hit his ear and fell straight to an opponent's feet. If Sunil tried to take the ball from a Prickly Gorse player, he missed it, his adversary fell over, the referee blew up for a foul and gave Sunil a lecture on fair play.

All the time they looked for that little figure on the touchline who would say, 'Put it out to Steve on the left,' or, 'Sam's behind you – leave it to him.' But she wasn't there, so they staggered along as if blindfolded. If Prickly Gorse were any good at all, they'd have won by more than 3–0.

Afterwards they sat in the minibus, silent and fed up.

'She'll be back next week, won't she, Dale?' said Sam.

'Perhaps,' said Dale. 'I don't know.'

The news came that St Boniface's had won. It meant that Firth Park had to win to be sure of the league. A draw was no good: St Boniface's had smashed their opponents 8–0, so their goal difference was better now. To lose would be complete disaster.

But disaster was what everyone in the Firth Park team expected. Unless . . . .

'She'll be all right, won't she?' they kept asking Dale.

'She may be,' was the answer.

'So she will be back, then?'

'I don't know. You never know with transplants. They might send her home again if the new liver isn't right for her.'

On Thursday Dale was away.

'He's gone to bring her back,' said Clive confidently.

But the confidence didn't last. There was a nasty feeling around that that wasn't the reason why he was absent.

By the day of the match Dale still wasn't back. Pete played in his place. They met, put their shirts on, laced up their boots and turned stricken, defeated faces towards Mr Gaynor.

'Snap out of this,' he said. 'You're a football team, not a nursery class. You should be ashamed of yourselves.'

'You don't understand,' mumbled Colin.

Mr Gaynor heard. 'What is there to understand?' he snapped. 'Just get out there and play. Janey would want you to. Win it for her.'

Easier said than done. They wandered aimlessly onto the pitch. They hoofed the ball half-heartedly around. They hardly heard the parents shouting, 'Come on, lads.'

Steve tried a weak practice shot at Trevor, who let it trickle into the net. He turned, bent down, picked it up, straightened, looked up – then cried out in joy.

Janey stood there, in woolly red hat and scarf, blue coat and warm black leggings.

Trevor shouted joyfully at the rest of the team. 'She's back!'

Suddenly their hearts lifted. They ran to the touchline by the goal where no spectators were and crowded round her.

It was definitely Janey. And she spoke, like always. 'I told you I'd be back, didn't I?'

'We knew you would,' said Steve and Delroy together.

'Right,' said Janey. 'Now listen. They're good, this team. They'll come at you hard to start with. They can move the ball around. Don't worry. Play it cool. You can keep them out. Get the ball out to Steve and Delroy. This lot are a bit weak down the middle. They don't like crosses. They'll be in trouble if Darren and Lee get on the end of a few.' She paused, then said, 'Come on. You can beat them.'

The referee blew his whistle. 'Thanks, Janey, we will,' they chorused and ran to their positions a new team.

She was right. St Boniface's were good and they came in hard. Attack after attack built up. Pete, in defence instead of Dale, was not finding it easy. But Colin and Winston covered him, Trevor was alert and St Boniface's didn't get the early goal they wanted. Only once did a Boniface forward get a clear shot on goal. Trevor leapt, pushed it round for a corner and looked to Janey for approval.

But he couldn't see her. 'She's joined the rest of the spectators,' he said to himself.

Still the pressure came. A Boniface forward burst through. Colin closed in on him. As he did so, he heard

139

Janey's voice, high, right in his ear. 'He'll push it out to your left.'

Colin was ready. He was moving that way before the forward could check. He cut the ball out and ran forward. Who should he aim for? Steve, Delroy, Lee?

'Look out,' came Janey's voice. 'There's someone behind you. Pass it to Pete on your right.'

Colin couldn't see Pete. But he slipped the ball to his right nevertheless and as the Boniface player came up beside him, he saw Pete's long clearance find Delroy.

'Remember what I said, Delroy,' Janey's voice came again. Delroy remembered well enough. He put in a low, hard cross – straight to Darren, who controlled it, eluded a Boniface defender and, while the goalkeeper wondered what to do, planted the ball in the net.

1–0, after a terrific counter-attack masterminded by Janey. In delight they turned to the touchline. There she was, standing on her own, very still, smiling slightly.

Half-time came: the score stayed the same. Mr Gaynor was delighted with them. Janey wasn't with him, but as they trooped back on the pitch she ran after them and came with them a little of the way. 'Don't slacken off,' she said. 'You haven't won it yet.'

And they hadn't. St Boniface's scored straight from the kick-off. Janey's message hadn't sunk in.

Now there was a real scrap. The teams tore into each other, after the vital winner. Two minutes from time, disaster happened. A cross came in from the Boniface right, deep into the penalty area. Pete went to meet the ball and clear. It bounced awkwardly and, before he could pull it away, hit him on the hand. The whistle blew at once. A penalty.

Dejectedly, the Firth Park team gathered round the edge of the area as the Boniface player placed the ball carefully on the spot. Trevor stood on his line, ready, trying to make up his mind which way to go.

'Trevor.' The voice came from behind him. Out of the corner of his eye, Trevor could see Janey standing by the goal. 'He'll shoot low to your right. Get down quickly. You'll smother the ball with no trouble.'

'OK, Janey,' Trevor said and tensed himself ready. The Boniface player ran up, shot – and Trevor dived, just as Janey had said. He hugged the ball to his jersey, got up and cleared.

The Firth Park players jumped up and down with joy. Steve and Winston ran forward to hug Trevor. Then they saw Janey. 'Keep playing,' she yelled.

The ball was bouncing free from Trevor's clearance. Darren, Delroy and Lee turned and streaked after it. Two defenders were left standing. Darren and Delroy got themselves into perfect positions. Panic crossed the goalkeeper's face: what should he do? Even as he made up his mind to run out and try to block Delroy, Lee pushed the ball to Darren, who slipped it into the net.

The whistle blew soon after. Firth Park had won the league after all. The boys could hardly speak for joy after all their troubles.

They didn't manage to talk to Janey, but they saw her standing a little way off, smiling to herself as they went up to collect the shield and their medals.

Once they had, they looked for her, but she seemed to have gone.

'Where is she?' cried Trevor.

'She won it for us,' said Pete.

'She said she'd be back and she was,' said Colin.

'But wait a minute,' said Winston. 'I don't get it. She was in hospital. She was having a transplant. You can't just get up and watch a football match straight after the day you've got a new liver.'

Trevor looked at him strangely. 'What are you saying, Winston?' he said.

'I don't know,' Winston replied. 'But . . . .'

'I know what he's saying,' said Steve. 'That wasn't Janey we saw. It was a . . . a . . .'

'Come on, Steve, say it,' said Pete.

'He means a ghost,' said Sunil. 'She died in the operation and that was her ghost.'

Everybody looked at Sunil.

'That's what I meant,' said Steve. 'Only I couldn't say it. The team meant so much to her that even though she'd just died, she had to come and see us win. I've read stories like that.'

Mr Gaynor was coming towards them.

'Look at him,' said Steve. 'I know what he's going to tell us.'

'So do I,' said Sunil. '"Boys," he'll say, "I had some bad news just before the kick-off. I knew I couldn't tell you until after the game."'

Nobody spoke. Sunil had to be right.

Mr Gaynor had reached them. They looked at him dumbly and tried to read his expression. They waited for him to speak and suddenly the shield and the medals were worthless, fit only to trample into the ground.

'Boys,' he said. 'I've got some news for you . . .'

Janey had woken. She was still woozy from the anaesthetic and tubes seemed to come out of her everywhere she looked. But Mum, Dad and Dale were there and so was the surgeon.

'The operation went brilliantly, Janey,' said the surgeon. 'There's no sign of the new liver being rejected and if everything keeps up as well as this you'll be fine and leading a proper life like everybody else.'

She smiled. 'Can I have some football boots when I'm fully better?' she said.

'The best money can buy,' said Mum.

'And a season ticket to Doncaster Belles,' said Dad.

Dale just looked at his sister and couldn't say a word.

There was something Janey had to know. 'How did Firth Park get on?' she asked.

'I don't know,' said Dad. 'We telephoned the school to tell them you were going to be all right, but the match was still going on.'

'We'll leave you now,' said the surgeon. 'You must get some more sleep.'

On her own, Janey felt happier than ever before in the whole of her life. Yes, she wanted to sleep now, properly, not brought about by strong anaesthetics. And when she woke up, she'd ask how the team got on. If only that incredibly real dream she'd had during the operation were true. But it couldn't have happened, surely, that Firth Park had won the league by beating St Boniface's 2–1, that Darren scored the first from Delroy's cross, that Trevor saved a penalty by diving to his right and Darren scored the winner in the last minute? Nor could things have turned out like that because she was there to tell them what to do. No, she was lying on an operating table miles away. It *was* just a dream, wasn't it? Even though it seemed *so* real.

Of course it was.

Pity. Without her they'd probably lost.

Still, there'd be other chances. Besides, it was time she started thinking about herself instead of those boys.

When she was better, up on her feet, strong and able to play football herself, she was going to start a girls-only team. And then, some time way in the future when she was *really* strong, she might play for the Doncaster Belles.

That would be the day.

STRIKERS
by Mat Coward

There's this . . . *thing* that Pep Fernandez does with the ball. The first time you see it, you think it's some kind of conjuring trick. But it's not; it's good football, and it gets results.

Give you an example: our third match of the season, Fox Lane second eleven (that's us) away to Alderman Jones reserves. Two minutes before half-time. Their striker, a big heavy bloke who's strong but a bit clumsy, is dispossessed just inside the area by our left-back, Mandy Cooke. She's very small, Mandy, and very quiet, and a truly gifted tackler – she uses her little feet like a surgeon uses a scalpel. She'll slice in there, cut the ball away from you, and pass it on, all before you've even noticed she's on the pitch.

Mandy taps the ball sideways, just a yard or so,

towards Mike Venables (nice guy, Official Team Comedian, but if you call him 'Terry' he'll make your face bleed), and Mike does what he always does when the ball comes near him: he shuts his eyes, pokes his tongue out, and kicks out with his left foot as hard as he can in the approximate direction of the opposing half.

Unlikely as it may sound, this system of Mike's does sometimes work, and on this occasion the ball lands absolutely dead at the feet of Fox Lane second eleven's one and only legendary net-stretcher, and my lifelong best friend, *ladees'n'genn'lmen put your hands together please* for Mister Pep Fernandez.

And that's when everyone on our side holds their breath, wondering if Pep's going to do his 'thing'.

Which he does . . .

I'm going to describe this in slow motion – even though, obviously, I've never actually seen it in slow motion – because, like most of the great bits of business you see on a soccer field, it's something that takes less time to do than it does to tell.

The ball hits the muddy grass just in front of Pep's right boot, a few yards out from the opposition area, over on the left of the box. Pep smiles – he's got his back to me, but I know he smiles, I've seen all this before, remember – and traps the still spinning leather with his heel. He feints his body to the right, as two defenders begin to close on him. And then comes the magic bit.

With the two defenders between him and the goal, hovering, trying to make themselves big, Pep walks away from the ball. Or at least, that's what it *looks* like. He dances a couple of skips to his left, and backwards – back towards our half. For a moment the ball appears to be unattended, sitting lonely and unloved on the turf. The defenders – well, they look as if someone's whacked them in the face with a sock full of cold porridge. They blink. Look at Pep. Look at the ball. Look at each other, and then back at their keeper. And then they sort of shrug, and rush forward.

Pep times his move with instinctive perfection. Suddenly, he's back on the ball, and the defenders realize (too late, because they're committed now) that he never really left it: it was all an illusion. And then he's *over* the ball, collecting it with his right instep, to banana it over the heads of both defenders, and way beyond the reach of the late-diving keeper.

Pep ends up on his back on the turf, laughing. The ball ends up in the far top corner of the net. It's a great moment – all our lot yelling '*Yeeeees!*' and punching the air and rushing up to thump Pep on the back as he clambers to his feet – and all their lot scratching their heads and arguing with each other and wondering just where on earth *that* came from.

I'm yelling louder than anyone, because Pep and I have been 100 per cent best mates, closer than brothers, ever since the day we first met – which was when we were about a month old (our mums used to work together). When Pep bangs in a great one like that, I feel almost as if I've scored it myself.

My name's Andy Callaghan, by the way. I'm the goalie.

After the break we were huddled on the sideline, getting a last-minute team talk from Mr Weiss, our coach. 'Try to give Pep a bit more ball,' he was saying. 'Their keeper's good, but he's not invincible. If we keep our nerve in midfield, concentrate on possession, we'll come out of this with points. All right?' He looked round at us, taking care to smile at every single player, and then he said: 'Above all, remember—'

We all knew what he was going to say next – what he always said – so we chorused it along with him: 'Play hard, play fair, and enjoy yourselves.'

The rain started to fall a few minutes into the second half, and pretty soon a sideways wind was blowing it straight into my face. There are times when I almost hate being a keeper, and this was one of them – stuck there shivering between the posts while the rain turned my specs into a blindfold.

Luckily, Mandy was on top form, harrying the Jones attack to great effect in her nippy way, rarely letting them get within sensible walloping distance of my goal. I made one pretty smart save in the seventy-fourth minute. A long aerial ball from the halfway line fell perfectly for Alderman Jones's tallest player, and he headed it strongly towards my upper left. But I got a clean fist to it and thumped it over the net for a corner. It looked more dramatic than it was: truth is, I like fielding headers from tall players, because their height makes it easier to guess where the ball's going to go.

The corner came to nothing, and we were feeling pretty pleased with ourselves. And it was then that the whistle blew. One long, hard, continuous blast. Which was puzzling, because the ball was out of play – our right-back, Malc, had gone to fetch it for a throw-in, and he's not the fastest fetcher on the planet. I looked over to where Mr Weiss had been standing, to see what he made of it, but all I could see was a knot of people, standing in a circle staring at the ground, and teachers running in all directions, shouting.

The ref came trotting over to me. 'Get your people off the pitch, and into the changing room,' he said.

'Sir?' I said, as he turned to trot away again. 'What's happened?'

'Your Mr Weiss has been taken ill. Looks like a heart attack. I'm very sorry, son – best thing you can do for him right now is get your lot organized. Ambulance is on its way. OK?'

In the minibus on the way home there was absolute silence, except for the sound of the windscreen wipers, and the rain drumming on the roof. Pep and I sat together at the back. We couldn't say anything. We just looked at each other and shook our heads, but I was glad to have him there. There are times when sitting in silence with a real friend is the only thing that keeps you in one piece.

We were met off the bus by Mr Hall – which was all we needed, quite frankly.

'You'll be relieved to hear that Mr Weiss is in a stable condition in hospital,' he told us. We were relieved to hear it, of course, but we'd have preferred to have heard it from someone we had even the tiniest fraction of a molecule of respect for. Which ruled out Mr Hall.

Hall ran the first eleven, and never made any secret of the fact that he thought we were, to put it bluntly, a load of rubbish which had no right to exist as a team. We'd learned to ignore him, pretty much. We *were* a team, the Fox Lane seconds, in every sense of the word. We stuck together, simple as that. We'd take criticism from our own coach, because Weissy was a really good bloke, he got on with everyone, he didn't have favourites and he didn't have unfavourites. But there was no way we were going to take any notice of an acid-mouthed old kid-hater like Hall.

What really wound him up was my mate Pep Fernandez. Pep had come on so much in the past year that he could easily have played for Mr Hall's firsts. But he chose to stay with us, and that got the veins throbbing in Hall's forehead, let me tell you.

Even then – on a tragic day like that – he couldn't resist a dig. 'Well then, Mr Fernandez,' he said, as we filed off the bus, Pep and I last off as always. 'Looks like your little toy-town team's going to be out of action for a while, doesn't it? Never mind – if you ever want a *proper* game of football, you know who to come and see, right?'

Pep said nothing in reply – said nothing very loudly, in fact – so after giving us both the benefit of one of his best sneers, Hall strode off, leaving us alone on the tarmac.

'Blimey!' I said to Pep. 'Can you believe that guy?'

'Yeah,' said Pep.

'Trying to poach you for the firsts – with Weissy lying in a hospital bed. Talk about out of order!'

'Yeah,' said Pep. I was hoping he'd say a bit more than just 'Yeah,' to be honest, but he obviously wasn't in the mood, and I didn't want to push him. You see, I knew perfectly well that Pep could never feel quite the same enthusiasm for the team as I did. He tried his best, but – well, the fact is that Fox Lane second eleven was pretty much my baby.

It happened like this. Originally, there was only one proper football team at the school, which meant that those of us who weren't good enough, or old enough, to represent the school, or who just weren't into the deadly serious, victory-or-death, train-every-night side of the game, never got the chance to play against other schools. Which struck me as unfair – especially as I knew of several other schools in the area who put out more than one team.

So one day I spoke to Mr Weiss about it – the one

teacher at the school who everyone really liked. 'Couldn't we have a team,' I said, 'for people like me who really love the game but are never going to play for the school? A team for people who want to play competitive football, but just for fun – if you see what I mean.'

Weissy wanted to know if I was serious. 'It's a good idea, Andy, but I'm not putting in loads of effort, giving up my spare time, for something that you lose interest in after a couple of weeks.'

To 'test my resolve' as he put it, Weissy made me do an assembly. I had to stand there for ten minutes, in front of everybody, explaining why the school needed a second eleven. I was dead nervous, but it all went pretty well. I made my presentation dressed up as a ref, with a whistle and everything, and I summed up my argument by saying, 'Why shouldn't people who aren't brilliant at football still get a chance to play? My sister's lousy at English, but they still let her speak it!'

That got a big laugh, even from the teachers (though not from my sister, admittedly), and the Fox Lane seconds played their first away match just three weeks later.

Mostly, the side's made up of people like me – football fanatics who would never be anywhere near good enough to get into the firsts. There are also two or three players who are good, but who prefer our more relaxed approach to the game – 'Play hard, have fun, don't cut your throat if you lose' sort of thing.

And then there's Pep. Well . . . as it turned out, the situation with Pep was more complicated than I realized.

'Right,' said Mr Hall. He looked around the assembly room at us – all the players from both Fox Lane teams. 'Let's get one thing straight from the start. This school has had an empty trophy cabinet for too long – and the drought ends now. Got it?'

A few of the first eleven crawlers nodded vigorously. I raised my eyebrows at Mandy. Mike rolled his eyes at me. We weren't impressed.

Mr Weiss had survived his heart attack, but he was very ill, and had retired from teaching. Just forty-eight hours after the abandoned match against Alderman Jones, Mr Hall had summoned us all to hear his 'plans for modernization of the football programme'.

'And we all know why Fox Lane hasn't been winning, don't we?' Hall continued, pacing up and down the little stage like a brigadier before a battle. 'Yes? Because, gentlemen and ladies, we have one team too many. Well, *not any more*.'

We stopped making daft faces at each other. This was serious.

As soon as he let us go, the second eleven met in an empty classroom.

'He's closing us down,' said Malc. 'I just can't believe it.'

'He can't just announce it like that, without consulting us first,' said Mandy.

'If he'd consulted us, we'd have said no,' Mike pointed out.

I was almost too upset and angry to speak. When I thought of all the trouble I'd gone to to get this team going. All the work Mr Weiss and the rest of the seconds had put into making it a success. Most of all, when I thought of how much fun we'd had, and how, if there was only one school team, most of us would never play in another match . . .

'We can't let him get away with it,' I said. 'We're not just accepting this.'

'Agreed,' said several voices. Then there was a moment's hush as we realized that we weren't really sure what it was we were agreeing to.

It was Mandy who broke the silence. Like I've said, she's small, but she's quick. 'That's settled then,' she said. 'We're going on strike.'

Pep spoke for the first time. 'Strike? How can we go on strike, if they're closing us down anyway?'

'No,' I said. 'Mandy's right. Hall said he's abolishing the seconds from the end of this term. It'd be a big embarrassment for the school if they had to tell other schools they couldn't play in the rest of this term's fixtures because their team was on strike.'

'Nice one,' said Mike. 'Not everyone in the staff room is a gung-ho pot-chaser like Hall. If they see we're serious about this, that we're really sticking together, I reckon they'll be forced to at least talk to us. I vote Yes.'

'Right,' said Mandy. 'All in favour?' There was some quiet cheering, as everyone in the room stuck their right arms in the air.

No: not everyone.

Pep was sitting on his hands, swinging his legs from a desk edge, and staring at the ground. Nobody else seemed to notice, but I looked right at him, willing him to look up at me. Eventually he did.

I didn't say anything. Pep could vote any way he liked, or not vote at all – that's democracy. But I would have given just about anything to see my best friend's arm in the air along with the rest.

After what seemed like a long moment Pep shrugged, and raised a limp, unenthusiastic hand about halfway between his shoulder and his ear.

I think it was right then that I fully understood for the first time that Pep was only in the seconds because of his friendship with me. And I didn't know what I thought about that.

SPORT FOR ALL! said the big banner (made by Mandy's brother who did Art GSCE). SECOND ELEVEN – NOT SECOND RATE! and LET US PLAY! said the smaller posters. Mandy and I were holding the banner; everyone else was waving a poster – except Pep, who hadn't turned up 'because it's my mum's birthday'. I suppose he'd forgotten that his mum's

157

birthday is the same day as my dad's – 23 December.

There was a governors' meeting taking place at the school, and we were picketing it, giving out a leaflet that Mike'd done on his PC, explaining our grievance. Even the head, Mrs Scott, was there – though not, I think, to express solidarity with our cause, but just so that she could tell all the governors as they arrived that she 'encouraged the pupils to take a lively interest in school affairs'.

It was Day Three of the Great Fox Lane Footie Strike, and things were going well. That week's match had already been cancelled, which we reckoned must have caused some red faces in the staff room, and a lot of kids and parents were supporting us – we were even getting discreet thumbs-up signs from some of the staff and governors.

'This'll be all over by next week,' said Mandy as we rolled up the banner after the meeting. 'I don't see how we can lose.'

'Definitely,' Mike agreed. 'We've already won the argument. I expect we'll have to compromise a bit, maybe play fewer matches or something, just so it doesn't look as if the school's backed down. But provided we stay solid – well, Mr Hall must know he's lost, yeah?'

The next day we found out that Mr Hall knew nothing of the sort.

'Andy!' Mike grabbed me in the dinner queue. 'Have you seen the team sheet?'

'Team sheet? We haven't got a game – we're on strike, remember? Derrr!'

Mike wasn't smiling. 'Not *our* team sheet, mate. The first eleven: it's just gone up on the board.'

I had a horrible feeling I knew what he was going to say next.

He nodded. 'I'm afraid so. Pep's playing for the firsts.'

'There must be some mistake,' I said. To be honest, it was the only thing I could think of to say. 'I'll talk to him.'

I forgot about lunch, and went looking for Pep. He wasn't in any of his usual places, which made my sinking feeling sink even further. I eventually tracked him down – he was sitting by the dustbins, reading a football mag. He must've heard me coming, but he didn't look up.

'You've betrayed us,' I said, going straight in with the hard tackle. I knew it sounded a bit dramatic, but – well, it was how I felt.

'Football's important to me,' said Pep, quietly, calmly, as if he was talking to a stranger. 'I hate not getting any football.'

'So do we all, Pep! That's what the whole strike's about!'

He didn't reply to that. Just sat there looking at me, as if he was waiting to get thumped – and as if getting thumped would be preferable to having an argument.

'Look, Pep,' I said, trying not to sound as angry as I

felt, 'if you're someone's mate, you stick with them. Right?'

'I'm under a lot of pressure from my parents. You know what they're—'

'Forget the excuses, Pep! We could all come up with excuses. Let's keep it simple. Friends stick together. If they don't, they're not friends. That's what the word *means*.'

'Oh yeah?' He stood up. Now he looked angry, and I wondered for a moment if my best friend and I were going to spill blood. 'It's all one-sided with you, Andy. I have to play in *your* football team, I have to support *your* strike, I have to give up *my* football for *your* sake! And you just take it for granted, don't you?' He stopped, sighed, folded up his magazine carefully and put it in his pocket. 'Look, Andy, I could say that friendship also means supporting a friend even when you think he's done something bad. But there's no point. You want to keep it simple? Fine – then I'm playing for the firsts and there's nothing more to be said.'

Pep stood up and walked away. I sat where he'd been sitting, and wondered how I'd lost my best friend just by doing what I thought was right.

'The good news is, Mandy and Gary both turned Hall down for the second time,' said Mike.

Mandy nodded. 'We were quite polite, but I think he got the message,' she said. 'We're sticking with the strike, we're sticking with the seconds.'

'That's good to know,' I said. 'But we still can't pretend that losing Pep hasn't knocked a big hole in the strike. It has. Now Mr Hall can show the head that we're not one hundred per cent united – it makes it less likely that they'll negotiate with us.'

The strike committee – the three of us – were meeting at my place. In the week since Pep's defection some of the others had begun to lose enthusiasm. When we'd picketed the staff meeting the previous day, there'd been more posters than strikers.

'But we're not giving up,' said Mandy. I couldn't tell from her voice whether it was a question or a statement. Bit of both, maybe.

'Pep scored in both his first two games for the firsts,' said Mike. 'Crucial match tomorrow. Lawrence Cup semi-final, at home to Park View. They've got a good chance – people say Pep's playing out of his skin.'

'Yeah, I heard,' I said. I didn't really want to think about that. I'd never imagined there'd be a Pep Fernandez goal that I wouldn't witness. But his brilliant form, now that he was playing with footballers of his own calibre, was the talk of the school.

The strike committee meeting broke up without much being resolved. We'd keep going, do another leaflet, try to get a letter in the local paper. The way we looked at it was, we had nothing to lose – and if we held out long enough, we could still win. Nobody was feeling all that optimistic any more, though.

★　　★　　★

I'm not sure how I ended up watching Pep's big game the next afternoon. I certainly didn't intend to go – I wasn't talking to him, and he wasn't talking to me, and I didn't care how well or badly his precious first eleven did. Maybe I sleepwalked there, after a stodgy lunch and a boring maths lesson.

Anyway, however it happened, I was there: I saw Pep score two goals (one a superb diving header from the left post, the other a frankly fluky kick-and-hope from outside the area), and with only five minutes to go, and Fox Lane leading 2–0, I was standing directly behind the opposition goal when Pep received the ball from a long pass, and I saw his face as he realized he was in position to secure his hat trick.

There was only one defender near enough to bother him, and Pep soon had him flummoxed with that 'Fernandez thing' I told you about earlier – dummying him into coming forward too early, so that Pep only had to swerve a little out of his line, and bang it home.

It was a certain goal. A hat trick in only his third first eleven appearance. He'd be captain by the end of the season, at this rate.

I couldn't help feeling excited. I was still angry with Pep for betraying the strike, and for putting his football above our friendship, but at that moment I was just swept away by the sheer thrill of watching my old mate dishing out the skill, lighting up a grey afternoon with his fireworks.

Everyone was shouting, and suddenly I heard one voice louder than any of the others : '*Go on Pep, mate! Let's have number three!*'

Pep looked up, and I realized with a shock that the voice was mine. Our eyes met. He looked surprised, excited and a bit embarrassed – and I suppose I looked the same.

And time stood still, as if someone had hit the pause button. People still argue about what happened next, and Pep prefers not to talk about it, but from where I was standing this is what I saw: Pep looked at me, looked around him, looked at the near-open goal before him . . .

. . . *flicked the ball up to chest height and caught it in his hands.*

Sound and motion returned to my world. People yelling, a whistle blowing again and again. And Pep Fernandez walking calmly off the field, past the opposition goal, stopping just a couple of yards away from me. He smiled, tossed me the ball, and kept on walking.

'What's going on here?' It was the ref, speaking to me since I was the one holding the ball.

'Don't know, sir,' I replied. 'Something he ate, maybe. Anyway, here's your ball back.'

The ref (an independent, from a third school) looked at me for a moment as if he couldn't decide whether I was bonkers or insolent, then he snorted angrily, took the ball, and restarted the match with a free kick against Fox Lane. I dare say the rule book has a chapter devoted to what to do when a star striker walks off the pitch carrying the ball just before scoring a hat trick – but if so, neither the ref nor anybody else present that day had read it.

I found Pep alone in the changing room, scraping mud off his boots with an old lolly stick. I shrugged at him, and he shrugged back at me. Did that mean we were talking again?

'You could tell them you were ill,' I suggested. 'Migraine. Stomach bug. Bitten by a radioactive spider that crawled out of a bunch of bananas in the supermarket.'

He shook his head. 'I don't think so.'

'Could work,' I said. 'They'll give you your place back. They won't believe you, but they'll pretend to believe you – for the good of the team. They want you that much.'

He just shrugged again, and carried on with the lolly stick – which I took to mean that his career in the firsts was now over, as far as he was concerned.

I sat down. Not too close, but closer than enemies sit.

'So,' I said, 'when did you change your mind?' Because I knew, and he knew I knew, that if he wasn't ill, then walking off like that could only mean one thing: Pep had rejoined the strike.

'I didn't,' he said, with a halfway grin. 'I never changed my mind about it. I knew you were right all along. I knew that the way we were treated was bad, I knew we were right to go on strike, I knew that if we stuck to it we'd win. Most of all, I knew you were right when you said that friends stick together.'

'Look,' I said, 'I might have been overdoing that line a bit—'

'No, listen,' he insisted. 'You were right. Friends *do* stick together. You were right, but the thing is, *I* wasn't wrong. If you're someone's mate then you're their mate even if they do something you think is bad. Even if they do something that you think shows they don't understand what being friends means.'

I couldn't argue with that. It was only what I'd been telling myself for the last week. I hadn't been listening to myself, that's the trouble.

'I can't live without football, Andy, you know that. A chance to play for the firsts, really show what I can do . . . it was hard to resist. And then you got me so wound up, I just thought – why not?'

'And now?'

'When I saw you'd come to the game to cheer me on – well, that meant that you still considered us friends, right?'

'Right,' I said. It did, I supposed, unless you preferred the 'sleepwalking' explanation.

'In which case,' said Pep, 'it was time for me to show you that I felt the same way.'

We shook hands – quite formally, like a pair of battling midfielders, threatened with yellow cards by a stern ref.

'Come on,' I said. 'We'd better go and rescue Mr Hall.'

'*Rescue* Hall?'

'Yeah – after you walked off, the head was having words with him. Looked like she was thinking of killing him!'

All that happened last year.

Mr Hall resigned as football coach, due to 'a recurring knee injury'. Fair enough: I'm not going to call him a liar, am I? Mrs Scott, the head, took over herself.

Mr Weiss never returned to teaching, but he does come along to watch us play sometimes.

Following the walk-off incident, Pep was suspended from all football for three weeks. This was reduced to one week, when a flu bug presented Mrs Scott with severe selection problems.

The Great Fox Lane Footie Strike was settled in our favour: the second eleven was reinstated, and continues to thrive. Mrs Scott told the school in assembly that it had all been 'an excellent practical lesson in civics', but the truth is *we* won and *they* lost. They won't mess us around like that again – not as long as we stick together.

Pep Fernandez never played again for the seconds. He offered to, but we all told him not to be daft. He was obviously happier in the firsts, and after all – that was what the strike was about, wasn't it? People being free to enjoy their sport. Mandy's taken his place up front, and she's doing well there.

This term Pep's captain of the first eleven, and their highest scorer. He hasn't had a hat trick yet, but I know he will one day. Maybe for a Premiership side, who knows? Maybe for England. Wherever it is, I'll be there. I won't be playing alongside him, obviously, but you'll still be able to spot me.

I'll be the one making the most noise: '*Yeeeeeeeeeeeessssssss!*'

THE DIRTY DOZEN
by Tony Bradman

When Robbie Jones rode into the park one summer Sunday morning and saw a team coming out of the pavilion, he knew it was love at first sight. He had always wanted to play in a real team, and he had seen lots before – but this was definitely the one for him.

They were kids of his own age, but they trotted towards the pitch in a line just like a Premiership side. Their green and black strip was pretty impressive, each player's shiny shirt bearing a number *and* a name. They had a proper coach, too – a big, red-faced, track-suited man with a very loud voice who got them doing lots of professional-looking warm-up exercises.

There were some dads on the touchline, along with a few mums and little brothers and sisters. There was also an older man with a clipboard. Robbie left his bike by a tree, and went over to ask him the team's name.

'Top Grove FC,' the man replied. 'They're playing Athletico Brockley. It's a pre-season friendly, though I'm hoping it'll be a good game . . .'

It wasn't. It was scrappy and unexciting, but Robbie didn't care. He was more interested in asking questions. Mr Clipboard was very helpful, and by the time the teams left the field – a scrambled goal gave Top Grove a 1–0 win – Robbie knew plenty about the team he wanted to join.

He knew, for instance, that they were playing in a new league, that Mr Clipboard was the league's secretary, that the big coach was a wealthy businessman called Mr Matthews, and that his son Duncan was captain.

Robbie took a deep breath, and headed for the Top Grove players.

'You were brilliant, Dunc!' Robbie heard somebody say, which was strange, thought Robbie. Duncan hadn't really had *that* good a game.

'Er . . . hi,' said Robbie nervously. The group fell silent, and turned to stare at him. 'I was just wondering if you needed any more players . . .'

'What school do you go to?' said Duncan, stepping forward.

'Sunny Bank,' mumbled Robbie, his heart sinking.

'Really?' said Duncan. He glanced at Robbie's battered old bike, then looked pointedly at Robbie's scuffed, non-label trainers. 'Actually, I think we've got all the players we need at the moment, haven't we, guys?'

Robbie heard somebody sniggering, and felt his cheeks burn.

He trudged away, past Mr Matthews and Mr Clipboard, who were arguing. Top Grove's opposition had pulled out of the next friendly: Mr Matthews wanted a replacement, and Mr Clipboard couldn't find one.

Robbie rode out of the park. It wasn't fair, he thought. OK, so Duncan Matthews was posh, and rich. But he could still have given him a chance . . .

Robbie brooded upstairs in his bedroom until Sunday lunch, and right through the meal, and afterwards while he sat in the front room between his mum and dad. Not that they noticed. They were busy arguing too.

'I'm fed up with you deciding what we watch on TV the whole time,' Mum was saying. 'If it isn't blasted men kicking a ball, it's blasted men running around shooting at each other. What *is* this rubbish, anyway?'

'It's called *The Dirty Dozen*,' Dad replied with a heavy sigh. 'And according to the *Cable TV Guide*, it's a classic. This American officer leads a team of nutters on a special mission behind enemy lines. Got it?'

Mum wittered on, but Robbie wasn't listening any more. The film had given him an idea. A team on a special mission . . . a dozen was a football team, plus substitute. A team in which *he* might play – and show

Top Grove what he could do! Robbie sat forward, suddenly very excited.

'See?' said Dad triumphantly. 'Robbie thinks it's good.'

Robbie remembered the row between Mr Matthews and Mr Clipboard – Top Grove didn't have any opponents next Sunday. Although they might . . . *if* he could get a team together. He focused on the screen. The film's hero was talking to the kind of trusted second-in-command heroes always have.

A picture of his best friend instantly flashed into Robbie's head. 'Just popping out to see Gary,' he said, and jumped up.

'Traitor,' muttered Dad as Mum grabbed the remote.

Robbie rode to Gary's house. Gary's big brother Ian answered the door. 'All right, Robbie?' he growled. Ian had hit puberty in a big way, and his vocal cords had travelled so far south he sounded as if he should be doing voice-overs for horror movie trailers. 'You'll find him upstairs.'

Robbie paused on the landing by his friend's room. He suddenly felt uneasy. What was he going to tell Gary? Robbie wasn't the only one who wanted to play proper football, he realized. Gary and his other mates did, too. They hated the fact that Sunny Bank didn't have a team. Maybe *they* would like the chance to show Top Grove what they could do . . .

Robbie was confident of his own ability – but why make things difficult? Why give himself lots of

competition? He'd played football in the school playground with his mates for years, so he knew some of
them could be pretty impressive. They might even look
better than him on the day . . .

No, it would be best to keep his plan secret, he
thought. He could tell Gary this was a one-off, a single
opportunity to play a proper game, but no more than
that. Then, if the plan worked, he could simply act
surprised.

So for the second time that day, Robbie took a deep
breath. He pushed open Gary's door. Gary turned to
smile at him, and Robbie experienced a slight, but
definite twinge of guilt. He almost managed to ignore
it, too.

'I'm not sure, Robbie,' said Gary. 'Just suppose we
could put a team together. Nobody we know has ever
played a proper game, have they? I don't even have any
proper boots. We'd probably get slaughtered.'

'Not necessarily,' Robbie replied. 'I bet we'd be
good.' Although hopefully not *too* good, he thought . . .
with the brilliant exception of one particular player.
'And you could always borrow some boots.'

'OK, so who's actually going to phone this Mr
Matthews to arrange the game?' Gary asked. 'He'll only
want to talk to an adult. Mind you, I suppose we could
always ask your dad. He likes football, doesn't he?'

'I'd rather not,' said Robbie hurriedly. 'And I, er . . .
think it's best if we don't involve our parents.'

Gary raised an eyebrow, then shrugged.

'We know someone who *sounds* like a grown-up, though,' Robbie added . . .

It didn't take much to persuade Ian – just a promise to get the phone number of a boy in their class, a boy whose older sister Ian fancied. Then, after a search in the phone book, and calls to the wrong Mr Matthewses, and a brief, loud conversation with the right one, the deed was done.

'There you go, lads' said Ian. 'Kick-off ten-thirty next Sunday morning.'

'*Yes!*' said Robbie, and raised a fist. He was on his way . . .

Robbie and Gary rang their mates the next morning. Everybody was up for the game, and Robbie soon had a list of twelve names, including his own and Gary's. Robbie decided to set up a training session, too. If the team did get slaughtered, he'd realized, *he* wouldn't be able to show his skills. So he'd need the lads to have a bit of basic organization, at least.

That Tuesday, Gary ticked everybody off on the list as they arrived – Wayne, Lefty, Luke, Big Dan, Billy, Jez, Ahmed, Willsy, Darren and Martin. They were all excited, and stood around chattering. Then the inevitable arguments started about who should play in what position.

This was something Robbie hadn't bargained for. He'd simply assumed he'd play in central midfield, his dream spot. But now he realized that unless he took control of the situation, he could end up playing anywhere.

'*Quiet!*' he yelled. Everybody fell silent and stared at him. 'This was my idea, so I'm in charge, and *I'll* decide who plays where.' There was some grumbling, but it soon died down. 'Right, Luke, you're in goal . . .'

It didn't take Robbie long to make his decisions. He knew everybody's strengths and weaknesses – who could shoot, who could head the ball, who could tackle. And, of course, he gave himself the position he wanted. He'd promised the lads a training session, so he set up a six-a-side game of attackers versus defenders, although it soon deteriorated into an aimless kick-about – which was OK by Robbie. Gary, however, thought otherwise.

'You'll have to be a bit tougher with us in tomorrow's session, Robbie,' he said when they found themselves marking each other. 'I mean, this is fun, but we're not really making much progress as a team, are we?'

'Tomorrow's session?' said Robbie uneasily.

'Maybe we could go to the library on the way home and get out some of those coaching videos for ideas,' said Gary. 'And some books, too.'

'I wasn't planning on us doing any more training,' said Robbie.

'You what?' said Gary. Then he laughed. 'You're joking, right?'

'Huh, can't fool you, can I, Gary?' said Robbie, and smiled stiffly.

So Robbie scheduled more sessions. They trained on Wednesday, on Thursday, and on Friday. Thanks to Gary and his coaching videos and manuals, they were more organized, too. They had a final session on Saturday morning, agreed to meet in the park at ten o'clock the next day, and went home.

Gary and Robbie rode their bikes together as far as Robbie's house.

'You know, Robbie, I've been thinking,' said Gary. 'It's funny how things turn out, isn't it? I mean, if you and I hadn't been made to sit next to each other in reception class, we might never have become friends.'

'No, I guess not,' said Robbie, wondering where this was leading.

'Then you probably wouldn't have asked me to play in this game,' Gary continued, 'and it could be the biggest, most exciting day of my life. So I just wanted to say . . . thanks, Robbie. Thanks for being such a good mate.'

'Don't mention it,' said Robbie quietly. 'Please, *don't* mention it . . .'

Gary gave him a puzzled look, then rode off down the street.

The next morning Robbie got up, had breakfast, put his kit in a Tesco's bag, and cycled off through drizzly rain to the park with it dangling from his handlebars. The other lads soon arrived, and so did Mr Clipboard.

'I take it you're Top Grove's mysterious opponents,'

he said, his eyes drifting over them, and finally coming to rest on Robbie. 'Hold on, don't I know you? Oh, never mind. If you'll just point me towards your coach . . .'

'Er . . . he can't make it today, I'm afraid,' said Robbie. Mostly because he doesn't actually exist, he thought. 'We're looking after ourselves.'

'I see,' said Mr Clipboard. 'This is all very irregular. First your coach contacts Top Grove direct, instead of me as he should have done, and now I find out he's not even here! Tell me, what's the *name* of your team?'

'Their coach didn't give me a name,' boomed a voice behind them. Mr Matthews had also arrived. 'To be frank, I don't care *what* they're called so long as they're changed and ready by ten-thirty. Can we get on with it?'

'I suppose so,' said Mr Clipboard crossly, much to Robbie's relief. 'Although there's no need to be so rude,' he muttered. 'This way, boys . . .'

Mr Clipboard directed Robbie and his mates into the pavilion, and to a big room that had benches round the walls, with coat-hooks above. There was a lot of nervous laughter as they got changed, and a few jokes at the expense of Mr Matthews. Then it was time for Robbie to lead them out.

The rain had stopped, but as Robbie ran onto the pitch he noticed it was quite muddy. It seemed bigger somehow, too, and it was strange to see the same scene as last week from such a different angle. There were the

dads and mums and little brothers and sisters standing
on the touchline . . .

And there were the Top Grove players in their shiny
black and green shirts, sniggering openly at him and the
rest of the lads. Robbie glanced at his mates' scruffy kit
– the different replica strips, the odd socks, the cheap
or borrowed boots – realized why, and felt his cheeks
burning again.

'Right, can I have the two captains, please?' somebody called out.

It was Mr Clipboard, and to Robbie's surprise he had
changed too, but into a proper referee's strip. Robbie
trotted over to him in the centre circle, and so did
Duncan Matthews.

Duncan stared at Robbie, then smirked. 'Well, well,'
he said. 'I wasn't expecting *you* back so soon. If you're
this keen to show me what you can do, maybe I should
give you a trial after all. On second thoughts, perhaps I
ought to see you play a bit first.'

'What's he talking about, Robbie?' said Gary.

Robbie turned round. Gary was standing nearby,
scowling fiercely at him. Robbie opened his mouth to
speak, but just then Mr Clipboard started talking about
the coin toss, and Robbie had to pay attention. Robbie
lost the toss, and Duncan chose to kick off. Mr
Clipboard placed the ball on the centre spot, and the
teams got into position for the start of the game.

'Listen, Gary . . .' said Robbie as he moved back into
midfield.

'Spare me the excuses,' Gary snapped. 'I *knew* there was something funny about this. Not wanting to do any more training . . . you set it all up so you could get into their team! Hah! Some friend *you* turned out to be.'

Mr Clipboard blew his whistle as Gary finished speaking, and the game began, which was just as well, thought Robbie. He didn't have a clue what to say. Gary had him bang to rights, and Robbie felt absolutely sick. He noticed Willsy and Ahmed and Jez scowling, so they must have heard too.

Then somebody barged past him, and he was sent flying.

'Whoops, sorry!' said Duncan. 'I hope I didn't wake you up . . .'

Robbie never forgot that first half, his introduction to proper football on a proper pitch. It was a total nightmare. Top Grove were unlucky not to score from their very first attack. Duncan took a pass from a midfielder on the edge of the box. If he'd hit the ball better, Luke would have had no chance. But his shot skidded wide, and Robbie started breathing again.

There was no let-up, though, and soon Top Grove were all over Robbie and the lads like a rash. Shots rained in on Luke's goal, and Robbie was amazed none of them went in. He and his teammates simply couldn't seem to get any possession, and spent their whole time chasing Top Grove players. This is ridiculous, thought Robbie at last, and stopped running.

He looked at his team. They were supposed to be

playing 4–4–2, with Wayne, Big Dan, Billy and Lefty across the back, Willsy, Ahmed, Gary and himself across the middle, and Martin and Jez upfront, with Darren as sub. But the team had completely lost its shape – they were continually out of position, and getting in each other's way. What a mess, thought Robbie.

And so far *he* had done nothing but miss tackles and fall over. He hadn't put in any good passes yet, or hit a decent shot. He'd hardly been in Top Grove's half, and Duncan just laughed when he was near him. There was another problem, too. The whole team seemed to know now what Gary had said, even Darren on the touchline, and they were all scowling.

Then, of course, the inevitable happened. As Robbie watched, a Top Grove attack built up on the right-hand side. He started running again as a Top Grove player put in a cross. Somebody got a head to it, the ball came down in the area, and a second later . . . it was bobbling over the line. Top Grove had scored, and Duncan raised his arms to the sky in triumph.

'Great goal, Duncan!' bellowed Mr Matthews. '*Smashing* goal!'

That's strange, thought Robbie. He was certain Duncan hadn't got the final touch. But everybody in the Top Grove team seemed happy to let him take the credit – and Robbie suddenly understood why. *They had to*. I bet Mr Matthews started the team for Duncan, he thought, and that was the price for getting your name on one of those shiny black and green shirts . . .

In fact, as Jez lost the ball from the re-start, Robbie realized that Top Grove FC probably existed because Duncan thought he was a good player and wanted to show off. He kept calling for the ball, and doing tricks with it, and playing up to the touchline. But then, thought Robbie, he had no right to criticize. Wasn't that more or less what *he* had been intending to do?

Instead of which he'd simply managed to upset his best friend, and his other mates. He remembered that word Dad had used: *traitor* . . . And in the end, what had it all been for? Robbie saw Duncan bustling one of his own teammates off the ball, and realized there could never be a place at Top Grove FC for truly good players, or anybody who wouldn't take orders.

So the whole thing had been a total waste of time and effort, Robbie thought bitterly. Worse than that, he'd made a real fool of himself . . .

A few moments later Mr Clipboard blew his whistle for half-time. Robbie's mates slowly gathered in the centre circle, and stood in a tight huddle with their backs to him. Top Grove headed for the touchline.

'Well, *you* were pretty useless,' said Duncan as he walked past Robbie with his players. 'But then I always thought you would be. I mean, what can you expect from someone who goes to a school like Sunny Bank?'

Robbie heard more sniggering as they walked away . . . and suddenly he felt very angry. Who the hell did Duncan Matthews think he was, talking to him like that? What made *him* so special? A father with enough money to *buy* him a team? It was time to take Duncan Matthews down a peg or two, he thought. Robbie turned and marched off towards his teammates.

'You all right, son?' said Mr Clipboard as Robbie went by him.

'I'm *fine*,' said Robbie grimly from between gritted teeth.

'Second half kicks off in five minutes . . .' said Mr Clipboard.

Robbie didn't reply. He kept on walking, and finally stopped near his mates. The huddle opened to reveal Gary at its heart. Ten pairs of stern, disapproving eyes glared fiercely at Robbie, and none of his friends spoke.

'I know what you're thinking,' said Robbie, 'and you've got every reason to hate me. I *did* set this whole thing up to get into Top Grove, and I'm really sorry. You're my mates, and I realize now I'd rather play with you than those creeps, OK? Even if it's only for one last half. So let's get out there and show them what the lads from Sunny Bank can *really* do.'

He didn't give them a chance to argue. He turned round and walked quickly towards the goal they'd be defending, and stood there kicking at the penalty spot. He noticed Mr Clipboard giving him a curious look, and also saw his mates talking to each other, and occasionally glancing in his direction. Eventually Mr Clipboard called for the second half to begin.

For a moment Robbie thought his mates weren't going to play . . . but the huddle broke up, and they drifted to their positions, Darren coming on for Billy, as they'd decided. Top Grove were ready, too. Mr Clipboard blew his whistle, and Jez tapped the ball to Martin. A Top Grove player came in for a tackle, and the ball squirted out to Duncan, who was smirking.

But this half it's going to be different, thought Robbie, streaking up to put in a tackle of his own. He swept the ball from Duncan's toes and surged beyond him. Duncan went down and appealed to the referee.

'No foul!' yelled Mr Clipboard, waving his arms. 'Play on!'

Robbie was on the edge of the Top Grove box now, their midfielders chasing him, their defenders looking nervous. He jigged past one, then laid the ball off to Martin, who thumped in a shot. The goalie smothered it.

'Keep your shape when they come forward, lads!' Robbie turned and yelled as the goalie rolled the ball to the nearest defender. He noticed with pleasure that Duncan wasn't smirking any more. '*Keep* . . . *your . . . shape!*'

They did, too, mostly because Robbie kept reminding them. Fuelled by anger, he tore all over the pitch, getting in tackles, continually harassing, pressuring the Top Grove players' first touch, encouraging his mates. They responded, too. They started talking to each other, calling for passes or cover, and making good runs off the ball when the team was in possession.

Top Grove didn't know what had hit them, and Robbie began to realize just how useful the training sessions and Gary's videos and manuals had been. The breakthrough must come soon, Robbie thought . . . and then it did.

Big Dan collected the ball in defence and hit it to Ahmed. He took it down the left-hand side into the corner, then turned in sharply, easily beating a defender, and drove the ball hard and low into the box. Robbie had timed to perfection his run from midfield, appeared suddenly in the crowded area, and met the cross sweetly on the half volley. One each.

Robbie didn't celebrate, but turned round to go back for Top Grove's re-start – and was promptly flattened by all his teammates, who had rushed up to mob him. All of them, that is, except Gary, Robbie noticed.

Their second goal came pretty quickly. Mr Matthews was bellowing at his team so much that they started to get desperate, and eventually Duncan brought Jez down on the edge of the box. Mr Clipboard gave a free kick. Willsy blasted a shot into the wall, the ball rebounded to Robbie, and from fully twenty-five yards he curled it round the leaping keeper into the net. 2–1.

But it wasn't the best moment. That came right at the end.

Wayne knocked a long ball up to Willsy, who flicked it on first time to Robbie. He looked round, and saw Duncan steaming in to close him down. Robbie waited, nutmegged him, and headed for goal. Gary raced in from midfield beside him. Robbie dummied one defender, then a second, and only had the keeper to beat for a hat trick. Now that *would* be something . . .

He knew he could do it, too. But he drew the keeper instead, and neatly laid the ball off for his best friend to score with a simple tap-in. 3–1 – and this time Gary was the first in the mob that rushed to flatten Robbie.

'I take it this means I'm forgiven,' Robbie said happily at last.

'Forgiven for what, exactly?' said Gary, grinning at him.

Robbie grinned back, and just then Mr Clipboard blew three blasts on his whistle for full-time. A ragged cheer went up from Robbie's mates, and he and Gary joined in, then high-fived each other with a loud . . . '*Yes!*'

Duncan and his team slunk away to a *very* red-faced Mr Matthews.

'Could I have a word, lads?' called out Mr Clipboard, jogging over. 'I thought your second-half performance was terrific. You're just the kind of team we want in the league, so I was wondering – would you like to join?'

'Well, I, er . . .' Robbie mumbled.

'Look, I've already guessed you don't really have a coach, but that doesn't matter,' said Mr Clipboard. 'I'll find you one, and a sponsor as well – if you promise to play like that against Top Grove a couple of times a season. It'll be worth it just to keep old Matthews quiet. Is it a deal?'

'It most definitely is,' said Robbie. Gary was nodding eagerly too.

'Good,' said Mr Clipboard. 'Here's my card – get your parents to give me a call tomorrow so we can set things in motion. Oh, and I *will* need a name for your team if I'm to plan your league fixtures. What's it to be?'

Robbie thought for a second. Sunny Bank United? Council Estate FC? No . . . then he looked at his victorious teammates. Their scruffy kit was covered in mud, and they were laughing and capering crazily for sheer joy.

'You can call us . . . the Dirty Dozen,' he said, and smiled.

It just seemed right, somehow.

THE END

TONY BRADMAN

Tony Bradman was born in London in 1954, and went to Cambridge University. After graduation he worked in the music press, becoming chief subeditor of *Music Week*, the music industry's flagship trade paper, in 1978.

In 1979 he joined *Parents* magazine, where he became deputy editor. In 1980 he launched their highly successful children's book pages and in 1985, *The Best Books for Babies Award*, which in its first year was a major promotion for the Book Marketing Council and was covered by BBC TV. He ran the award for six years, and went freelance as a children's author in 1987. He has written for a number of newspapers and magazines, and appeared on children's book related programmes on both TV and radio. He reviews children's books regularly for *The Daily Telegraph*, and has edited a number of highly successful anthologies of stories and poetry for children published by Corgi Books. These include two previous football collections, *Football Fever* and *Football Fever 2*, as well as *Gripping War Stories*, *Fantastic Space Stories*, *Amazing Adventure Stories*, *Incredibly Creepy Stories*, *Sensational Cyber Stories* and, most recently, *Phenomenal Future Stories*.

Tony Bradman is married, and lives in London with his wife, three children, and a very tired word-processor.